Scrat[ching]

In The

Wry

Rob Little

In memory of Patricia, my wife of 50 years.

Special thanks to my daughter Louise for creating the interesting cover.

I will send a donation from every book sale to the Nicola Murray Foundation Ovarian Cancer Charity.

A Scratcher in the Wry

Table of Contents

Short Stories

Table of Contents

My Falklands Times
A Widow Recalls

In my nightmares, I see the bullet that kills John. Spread-eagled, in a water-filled foxhole, in his camouflage gear, the flashes from the endless field artillery barrage illuminate his blackened face. I recognise him from his stubborn jaw line and, shining from his eyes, the excitement of combat and the pride of fighting alongside his mates of 2nd Para. A part of my mind tries to protect me, creating blank periods - which never last - the sniper's bullet always blasts from the darkness, silently spinning, towards John's head. The sound of shattering bone, the top of John's head erupting, his brains flying out like so much mincemeat, always awakens me, my head exploding, screaming uncontrollably.

John was a paratrooper with The 2nd Battalion The Parachute Regiment and died on the 28th May 1982 in the fighting at Goose Green, a battle of the Falklands War. On the same day, Colonel H. Jones died heroically, reports said

I was a war widow and our teenage son was fatherless. I was distraught and wept rivers. But the grieving had to stop - and life had to go on - all those around me said, it must.

In January, this twenty-fifth anniversary year of the Falklands War, I joined the cruise ship Sunny, which was calling at the islands on a voyage around South America. It was time to visit John's Grave, in the British War Cemetery at Port San Carlos.

It was dull and overcast when I first saw Sunny, at her berth in Southampton Docks. The cruise liner's superstructure was gleaming white; painted on its bow, a large face, with lips of brilliant red, smiled to make us cruisers feel cheery.

The ferry, Norland, had shipped 2nd Para to the Falklands. John had told me, in one of the few letters he wrote to me whilst aboard, that conditions were cramped, the food worse than in the Aldershot mess. The Sunny carried its 2000 passengers in luxurious surroundings not found on many ships.

I saw the Norland sailing to join the task force, on television; John hadn't wanted to see me upset on the dockside. That day, streamers, stretching between Para and loved one's fingers, had tightened, then parted, and had fallen slowly, in ringlets, into the Solent. A military band played 'Sailing' – how I still hate that number.

Sunny sailed at 18:30, while half the passengers were at dinner. Dinner was, I found, as advertised: fine dining, and ever so dress-size-increasing tempting.

I was glad that I had chosen an early sitting. At 20:30, as we rounded the Isle of Wight, the gales had increased to storm force ten and the ship, for all her size, began pitching and burying her jolly bow into deepening troughs.

It was an uncomfortable night for all aboard.

By morning, the seas were down a bit. Next day, Sunny entered the Bay of Biscay, which was grey, but mercifully calm. When Cape Finisterre was on her port beam, the skies brightened, some sun-lovers sprawling in swimming attire on deck chairs.

Nearing the Equator, I was keeping my eyes open for a member of that elusive and rapidly disappearing species: Albert Ross. This was how John had humorously described, in his final letter, the first albatross to greet Norland.

Sailing across glassy seas now, I wondered how it was for John and his mates of 2nd Para, during their month-long voyage south: there would have been little entertainment for them, other than what they created themselves. Would the fictitious sighting of a sea creature have listed the ship, if the whole battalion flocked to one side of it for a look? Even brave men would need such diversions. And as they ventured further south, would *their* minds concoct nightmares? Would they see themselves dying; see the bullets ripping into them; see and hear the grenades and shells exploding in their midst; the screams of mates hopelessly injured or the sight of them blown to bits?

Some ports of call on the way to the Falklands were hugely interesting: Rio, its carnival, the spectacle and the sounds, perhaps the most memorable.

I awoke in Buenos Aires with Sunny already berthed alongside the Cruise Terminal. On the dockside, a brass band was playing 'Don't cry for me Argentina'. It was a more entertaining offering. In

March 1982, government-inspired demonstrators ensured 'Malvinas is Argentinas' was top of their pops.

Poor thinking had me take a taxi and venture alone into the city centre. I saw it as a challenge; perhaps an opportunity to remove any latent anger pangs I felt over John's death. If a middle-aged man clumsily brushed past me on a street, would I think it him who had killed John? Would I vent my rage, swing a handbag; make to claw his eyes out, a woman thing. Would I look a complete and utter fool, but feel all the better for it? If a mentally unstable low-life, a man suffering the traumas of the war, approached me begging, would I knock him to the ground and stand over him, a foot on his head - my act of revenge? Nothing like that happened. I found the people courteous, the city vibrant.

We left Buenos Aires for the Falklands and were then 3 days at sea. Although it was summertime down there, the sea became choppy and a chill southerly wind was always blowing.

On the morning of landfall Falklands, I awoke and looked through the porthole of my cabin. Sunny was slowly sailing up San Carlos Water, the surrounding bleak hills and shoreline covered in tussac-grass clumps, heather and dotted with disinterested sheep. During breakfast, I heard the clatter of the anchor dropping and heavy chain paying out. A few minutes later, the lifeboat derricks rumbled into life as seamen lowered the tenders into the water. I felt tense. My tummy muscles had tightened. I had no appetite. I knew it would be a long day, so I ate what I could. The small group visiting war graves were to be the first passengers the tenders took ashore.

Safely ashore, I stood with the group on a ridge overlooking the inlet. A veering wind was howling about us, speeding black clouds in several directions at once, and moving Sunny on her anchor. Petrels, gulls and a lone albatross soared away as blasts caught them. Penguins slipped out of wave tops onto sand, became upright, stood gawping for a moment and then waddled off, up well-flippered paths. A seal poked its head from the water and glared at us.

I closed my eyes to picture the scene on the night of April 21st 1982, the date of the landings at San Carlos. I had seen some TV documentaries and had heard reports of the weather conditions, which aided my recall. Some Royal Navy ships were standing by as

Norland, Europic Ferry and Canberra discharged commandos, 2nd and 3rd Para and equipment. It was freezing, with gale-driven, horizontal sleet falling. 2nd Para, heavily laden with kit, were boarding landing craft using Norland's stern ramp. I followed their hairy, wave-tossed ride to (Blue beach) and shivered feeling their fears that the Argentineans had them in their sights, ready to fire shells in their direction, blow all aboard to pieces, before reaching the shore.

Miraculously, news channels reported, 2nd Para landed safely, seasickness and wet feet the main complaint.

I turned to face Sussex Mountain. Beneath its summit, 2nd Para had dug in and were in their holes for a week before the battle for Goose Green. A few sheep grazed there, the area free of land mines.

The M.O.D repatriated most of 2nd Para's dead after the war ended. John was one of those who wanted interment where he fell. Months later, undertakers moved his body to the War Cemetery at Port San Carlos. I had never thought it selfish of him. In my book, he was a hero and heroes had those rights. Had his body come home, though, and buried in a family plot, with the military honours it deserved, I would have kept his grave as neat and tidy as the one in the cemetery I walked into that day.

John's grave was at the end of a row. A sob rose quickly, my chest heaved and tears flowed as I approached and saw, marked in black on the headstone of Orton Scar limestone - Pte John Blanks, 2nd Battalion The Parachute Regiment. 'It is Emily, John. I dearly love you and still miss you.' The anguished prose came spurting out, quite naturally, as if I was standing there with John close enough to hear me. The wind gusting over the cemetery wall was whipping away my words, up onto Sussex Mountain, away from the other visitors showing their grief. Was John's ghost listening? Was his spirit and those of his dead mates still parading up there on the slopes, awaiting orders to march home?

I had brought a white rose from the Sunny and laid it on the grass, the green, green grass of John's eternal home. The wind began tugging at the petals as I stood; they would wither, fall and grow old, as we grow old - but not John - or my love for him.

A minibus took the group from there to the Goose Green settlement. In a typical, wrinkly-tin-roofed Falkland's home, a thankful islander offered us soft drinks and tea. Diddle Dee jam, made from a small red berry and a Falkland speciality, we sampled on buttered scones. The islander gave us his account of the Argentinean occupation; how they had feared for their lives when a senior army officer threatened to line them up and machine-gun them; how much they appreciated Mrs Thatcher for sending the task force. And through it all, knowing the fighting qualities of the British Forces, how the islanders never gave up hope of liberation.

Then we took another narrow road to the equally well kept but much larger Argentinean War Cemetery at Darwin. There, standing silently holding hands, after laying a floral wreath on a grave, were an elderly Argentinean couple. There were nods of greeting between us, wet eyes, but no words.

That Bloody Cat's Back

True, it was a shock when the mother-in-law's toes suddenly curled, connecting big time with the pail. It was a further shock when my missis, Sadie, and I realised she was uninsured and we had to fork out for the funeral. Cremation was the cheapest option so we took the old girl one last journey down that route. Her final journey was back to our mantelpiece in a cardboard urn.

Sadie's mum had lived in a council house for years. Her furniture was tat, old; nobody wanted any of it so we paid a white-van man to cart it to the rubbish tip. I wasn't too pleased coughing up for that outcome, either.

The only heirloom bequeathed to us was her manky, straggly-haired ginger cat. I was sure she had a touch of lion in her makeup, but she boasted the most popular name in moggiedom: Kitty.

Of course, Kitty took to Sadie; seemed to hate me. Whenever I wanted to sit next to Sadie, on the settee, to snuggle close, share a bottle of wine or watch TV, Bloody Kitty leapt between us and wouldn't budge her feline backside. Kitty was asking for trouble!

When she brought her noxious anal gland with its oily, stinking chemical warfare onto the battlefield to attack me, move me from my rightful place next to my missis, it was the final straw.

The first opportunity to get rid of the beast, I promised myself I'd take.

That occasion arose one Friday night. It was usual that Sadie ironed shirts and stuff so that I had something to look smart wearing down the pub of a weekend night. A couple of pints with my mates were my only relaxation outside the home of any week; small reward for my job heaving wheelie bins onto the hoist at the back of the garbage truck.

Kitty was lying happily asleep, purring gently on my settee spot. She could have been dreaming of sexual molestation by one of the marauding Tomcats stalking the alleyways near our house after dark. An abdominal scar showed she had had been spayed, but I didn't know if she got laid regular, when she left the house late at night. Perhaps she just went to perform her ablutions or mouse. More likely, she was planning her next attack on me, armed with something akin to Agent Orange, phosgene or mustard gas.

I snatched up an Aldi bag from the kitchen, crept close to Kitty, picked her up by her neck scruff and rammed her into the bag, before she realised what was happening.

Out the back door I flew, tying a knot in the bag as I went, sealing Kitty inside. My car was a Volkswagen Beetle, the one with the boot up front. I unlatched the boot lid and tossed in the bag, making sure it bounced a couple of times before it hit the back. I heard a loud, painful squeal. It pleased me.

There were big acreage fields not five minutes from our house. I considered one of them *the* ideal place to dump this germ-warfare exponent. In the potato field, the shaws were high, but the drills I could walk easily along until I quickly reached the field middle.

I dumped the bag there, unopened, leaving the beast to perish. Perhaps a fox or dog would rip the bag open and tear Kitty to pieces, slowly. I wished I'd taken a spade with me. A small burial would have gone unnoticed.

Back home ten minutes later, I pushed open the living room door to find Sadie sitting on the settee with Kitty, looking not the least discontented, laid across her lap.

How she had escaped and returned home safely as quickly I couldn't work out. I was stunned.

Other opportunities would arise, I was sure; next time I'd use a stronger bag, secure it better and the dumping site would be at least ten miles from our house.

When Sadie took a bath, she usually languished in it, reading a book for at least an hour, topping up with hot water to keep warm. Early Sunday evening was her usual time and I prepared for a Sabbath moggienapping.

The bags the council sell for 50p a go for householders in which to collect additional rubbish are extra strong. If I doubled the bags up, tied the beast's legs up with Gaffa tape, surely there would be no escape from my next attempt.

Early evening, Kitty had drifted off, her light snores catching my hearing. A simple snatch and a quick flick around the front paws

11

with a length of the tape trapped her. I even wrapped some tape around her jaws for good measure, ensuring she couldn't bite her way out, as it seems she must have done that the last time.

In the bag, she did a bit of birling, but no claws broke through. On hitting the rear of the boot with a resounding thump, I imagined, but for the tape clamping her meowing jaws together, she screamed in pain, such was the strength in my throw as I hurled her onto the hard metal surface.

I drove like crazy, swinging the car around bends, giving Kitty the last 'ride of her life', rattling her from side to side off the metalwork. A wood, some 10 miles distance, was my destination.

I had the Gaffa tape with me. I scrambled through the twilight of the wood. Near its centre, I found a tree with a branch just above head height. I lashed the bag to it; there was no movement inside. Kitty might be dead already. I wished. Then I safely made my way out, without breaking my neck tripping over twisted and raised root formations.

As I parked up outside our house, the bathroom light was out, the bedroom light on. Sadie would dry herself off there, dress in a nightgown and lash on some 'I'll make you want me' perfume, before joining me on the settee. Sunday used to be our lovemaking night. We had always looked forward to these sessions. Then Kitty arrived. Her foul-smelling squirting, every time I'd tried to get close to Sadie, would put a skunk off any form of sexual activity.

Now I had accomplished mission impossible. I'd rid the house of Kitty. Tonight could be a night to remember.

As I entered the hallway, Sadie was halfway down the stairs, Kitty in her arms, some whiskers missing where she had torn the tape off her face.

The sight dropped my jaw. I was flabbergasted.

I was more determined than ever that Kitty had to go. The cat was making an absolute fool out of me. However, only I knew that, and I wasn't about to share the information with anyone.

Each Wednesday, evening session, Sadie went to the bingo with pals. An afternoon telephone call for Sadie confirmed the venue for that night. I considered her lengthy absence would give me the opportunity to drive far from the beaten track.

I marshalled my thoughts: somewhere up a fell, in the Lake District, 60 miles from Annan, at least, would be an appropriate, out-of-the-way location, dumping site, from where an unwanted moggie couldn't possibly find its way home.

The second hand shop had a strong and secure cat-proof-looking holdall. I bought it cheaply, secreting it in the car boot. The small lock I kept in a pocket. There'd be no escape next time.

Wednesday evening at 6p.m., Sadie's lift arrived. I'd have at least 4 hours to get to my destination and be home before her. I was in trapping mode by 6.05 p.m.

Kitty was sitting contentedly on the settee as I approached her. She stood up, arched her back, raised her hackles and bared her teeth as she viewed my intent. I held the holdall open-side down and leapt towards her, pushing it down over her, securing her within. The zip closed easily and the lock clicked into place sharply: job done.

Further map reading had pointed me in the direction of the River Derwent as an ideal dumping site. The river flowed towards the Irish Sea, rising from the small Styhead tarn, high in the Lake District. I memorised the route to get to the tarn from an old map. I would take the M6 as far as Penrith, then turn west along the A66 towards the Lakes, then the B5289 into the hills.

The Derwent tumbled through Borrowdale Valley, before entering Derwentwater, continued westwards, through Lake Bassenthwaite and out into the Isel Valley. The Derwent flowed from the Lake District to Cockermouth, the River Cocker joining there, adding to the already significant stream. I considered a voyage of this magnitude was enough to confuse any cat with senses limited so entombed, if it had not already drowned in a waterlogged holdall, before swirling out into the Irish Sea at Workington.

This was the ultimate one-way ticket for any unwanted moggie, of that I was sure!

By 8 p.m., I was high in the Lakeland fells, on the track to the tarn. Swinging round a bend, I saw the small stretch of water ahead. I travelled along its edge until I saw a bridge. Beneath the bridge, tarn

13

water left in a strong cascade, splashing over glistening rocks. It was not quite in an impressive waterfall yet, but crashing noises coming from around the bend, up ahead, hinted of a stronger flow there, possibly over a high escarpment.

I swung the holdall around my head 50 times, enough to stun any moggie head blessed with innate, home-finding abilities, then dropped it into the gurgling water to watch it plummet away to disappear beneath a covering of foam.

It got dark quickly and I still cannot remember where I took the wrong turning. At 10 p.m., I was in a cul-de-sac: an old slate quarry at the end of some godforsaken trail, Herdwick sheep all around, watching me, bemusedly.

'I panicked, that's for sure. I checked my mobile to see if it had a signal. It was weak, but it was there. I rang home. Sadie answered. 'Is Kitty there,' I asked.

'Yes, she's here. However, I think she has been out fighting with the Toms. All her claws are missing and her paws are raw. She has no whiskers. Some teeth are missing, as is one ear. She looks a bit wet, confused and angry to me.'

'Can you put her on the phone for me?' I asked, 'I'm lost!'

Spot

It would demean Spot's worth and my memory of him if I said he was just 'the dog' and was not once a valued member of the Little family.

Spot provided food. He protected. He was a personality with wonderful senses. The words that I use in an earnest attempt to describe Spot can never convey the true significance of his canine existence.

His face was black and white with tinges of brown, a typical Border-collie spaniel-cross face that oozed intelligence and poise. All healthy dogs have cool black noses, as Spot had when it wasn't rent, bloody and painful from the bites rats, the scourge he was repeatedly obliged to eradicate for local farmers, inflicted on him as they strove to escape his jaws.

His ears were forever alert for the rustle of animals in hedgerows or long grass and he listened in to human talk. He stirred quickly and pranced in a flurry of enthusiasm when hearing a key word like walk…and reacted quicker still on hearing the word 'rabbits.'

Truly super-loyal, he had the innate canine instinct to hunt and he read minds. That these doggy traits were not lost to the world, he spread his genes prodigiously.

Unfussy and quiet in the cottage, he knew his place. His bed was an old rug behind granddad's armchair. When my grandparents retired for the night, but before they doused the light, Spot would place his head on the edge of their bed, where granddad would rub his ears and pat his head, such was the affection they felt for each other.

My father, in the Army during the war, arrived home on leave only occasionally, often unexpectedly. Spot seemed to know these days and granny looked out for them, often remarking, 'Bill must be coming home today, that's the third time Spot's been to the road end.'

His tail wagging and on high alert, Spot did pay many visits to the loaning leading to the main road bus route on such days. A child then, I can still picture his reaction on seeing the bus pull up and a figure emerge. Standing high on fidgety legs, ears erect, eyes rapt, he'd give a small howl of excitement on seeing a blurry figure in the distance. When recognition came, his doubts gone, how he'd speed up the loaning showing the pent-up whirl of doggy welcome he reserved only for his master.

Protective, and ready for combat he'd growl at the stranger knocking on the door and at any other dog that had only thought about intruding into his territory. He loved the bitches and when they came into heat, he'd mount them as natural as you like. Whether it was up the farm track, in the road, in front of the cottages to the mirth of the male villagers and the screams of the women, he didn't care, just did the job well. A bitch fox he'd chase and run alongside, but not mouth and bring down; she was just a strange game to him.

During and after the war, rabbit meat played an important part in the villager's diet. Cooked variously as curries, stews, roasts and in pies, its popularity lasted until the hideous, man-manufactured rabbit affliction myxomatosis appeared some years later, making them scarce and any survivors being unpalatable to sensitive humans. It was as natural for us to spend our weekends healthily hunting rabbits, as it is today to assume the easy role of the couch potato and watch sport on TV.

In my father's company, Spot, the ferret in its carrying pouch, or the gun on father's shoulder, in the days of which my memories are now duller, I wandered the Solway shores and across farmer's fields, down along hedgerows, looking for any likely warren. Spot always knew the nature of the hunt. With a solitary sniff at a burrow, he spotted the ones certain to house a trembling bunny.

Spot was always first to know of any rabbits in residence. He'd swiftly go around the warren's holes in a frenzy of sniffing, eager to communicate the tell tale signs to us with rapid tail wags,

Important positioning of the catching nets over the boltholes quickly completed, my father would remove the ferret from the pouch and put it into the burrow, setting it off on its underground exploration, we awaiting the fleeing rabbits. Sometimes the thwack of rabbit's back feet beating out 'danger is approaching' on the ground forewarned other rabbits. The sound also told us of the closeness of the bolt and the confirmation of Spot's prediction as he leapt about in excitement and madly prance, ears erect, tail ever circling, watching, waiting.

Sometimes suddenly, and in a flurry, a flash of brown closely following a daub of yellow signalled a rabbit leaving a bolt with the ferret in close pursuit if not already attached to it by sharp teeth. The rabbit would hit the net, which would close around it, tight, captured. Quickly another net replaced that one. Other times the rabbit might luckily choose a hole unsighted to us, perhaps obscured beneath a shield of gorse and left un-netted, and make good its escape. Where there was one rabbit, country lore told us, there would be another. Quickly we'd cover that hole too.

Hunting in the turnip and potato fields, Spot would leap high over the shaws and flush out any rabbit or hare lurking there, towards the edges of the field and the waiting gun. He would stop and listen for the telltale signs, the shaws moving, the scurrying of the heart bursting escape attempt. Then he'd part the shaws and with speed disappear beneath them on the chase.

When visiting snares set the previous day for overnight catches, he knew every placement. Any snared rabbit we sent to its afterlife easily and painlessly. One hand gripped its neck and the other pulled on its back legs. We found rabbit legs handy things too. A slit between bone and tendon above the foot of a back leg, then the other back foot laced through the slit, turned it into a good handle.

In wintertime, onto the farms around the village, came 'the mill'. Hulking, reeking, coal burning, monsters pulled threshing mills— until replaced by combine harvesters that did the complete job out in the fields— appeared often and puffed through the village to thresh the grain from the straw that stood in a pile of stacks built on the edges of the fields. A belt that flapped noisily linked the tractor unit drive wheel to the thresher unit wheel, transferring the power required to turn the thresher's mechanical innards that hummed as they flailed.

Two of the village's hardiest women, and I can include *my* mother among them, stood on top of the thresher and a worker tossed sheaves of corn up to them. They cut and removed the twine binding the sheaf and handed the sheaf to another worker who fed it into the thresher's maw. Its progress through the thresher remains a mystery to me to this day, but from one exit came the straw, stripped of its grain, to cascade into the baler, which automatically tied it up with wire into oblong bales. Farmhands removed it to be stacked again for cattle bedding and feeding. The grain, already pre-graded for size, poured out of shoots into sacks. Chaff blew free and many poor villagers filled their mattresses with it. My mother was one.

Special requests went out for 'super ratter's' presence at a mill, though his efforts went unacknowledged until the workers reached the lower levels of the stack. As sheaves disappeared upwards onto the thresher, rats, mice and their nests were uncovered. Spot would display his courage, his appetite, and not a little confusion. He had to consider the choice of many mouthfuls of warm, and I suppose succulent to him, baby rats and mice as they tumbled from the stack, over the chase of an adult rat. His reward for a rat chase might be a painful nip on the end of his nose, as the rat turned when he went in for the kill. But his instinct was for the rat, he caught many, the many that turned to face him, and he'd the scars to prove it. He'd throw a rat that had bitten into his nose and clung on to it, into the air, catch it in his teeth on the way down and shake it to death with relish. The rips on his nose was the badge of courage and endeavour worn by 'super ratter'.

Often he returned home weary from his efforts, his nose bloody and painful, and his belly taut with mouse meat He would sleep, perhaps not so soundly, but his digestion would soon take care of the meal, and his wounds would mend quickly.

Memories of him fade, but I can see him now whenever I want to, in picture form, alas, a serene presence amongst the many family portraits hanging on my parent's wall. It is the rightful place for our hero. The picture of stillness that we cherish is that of 'the dog', NO, the SPOT we once knew.

Cor, Love A Duck

Henrietta, it's late on Saturday night. I feel carefree, my head giddy with alcohol. I am reflecting as I await your arrival, my darling, upon our love and our impossible dream.

Angling at the pond began last year as the gusting winds of early March trumpeted springtime's first thrusts. Fragrant hawthorn blossom blew hither and thither, the frost-hardened ground alive with its wispy, frantic fling. New leaves were sprouting. Crows, with great outburst of cawing, busily built or refurbished nests high in surrounding trees. The raucous cries of worm-hungry birds following the plough, filtered from a nearby field. Sheep bleated in the meadows, their offspring at play. Hares reeled and sparred in short grass, obsessed with their mad March thing.

Henrietta, I sat by the water's edge on many Saturdays, on my small stool, fishing rod by my side, watching my float bobbing in the circles left by fish breaking the pond's surface. Many handfuls of wriggling maggots I threw towards my favourite lies, tempting the pathetic fish I returned to the water before the end of day. A monster pike, no figment of anglers' exaggerations, lurked hidden beneath some telltale ripples, refusing to take my bait. Those happy days filled me with nature's wonders, as did you Henrietta.

By the second Saturday, several well-known faces had returned to grace the pond with their presence. Your mum, a proud and beautifully marked duck, she was there. The drake known to us anglers as Sir Francis had noticed her, showed interest in her. Mooched food stuffed the tough old bird's crop and he was bursting of his own importance. The ugly, bullying, variegated drake was wild-eyed, rampant, sex-mad, a mongrel of the species.

According to other anglers, fifty-seven varieties of duck were in his breeding, and he had fathered many of the ducklings hatched at the pond each year. Sir Francis domineered, lorded over his drakedom, causing the glorious racket that stirred the air during the many squawking, breast-to-breast skirmishes he fought over mating partners and food.

Within weeks, a world of waterfowl, too many varieties to remember, Henrietta, were nesting cosily on the small island in the pond's centre, patiently sitting on their eggs. Males of the species dabbled for food, but woe betides the bird eyeing a titbit claimed by the greedy Sir Francis.

In May, mother ducks encouraged their hatchlings into the water. That is when I first saw you, Henrietta; you popped up from nowhere, like a water nymph, bright, mysterious, inquisitive, a bundle of white fluff, standing out in the variegated flotilla paddling furiously behind your mother.

My eyes never left you, Henrietta. I worried about you, my pearl in peril. The monster pike, you see, took ducklings easily and had them for his tea. You were so different to the hoi polloi; you were white Henrietta, whiter than the driven snow that piled up against the gable end of my home during winter snowstorms.

As you grew, I had to defend you. Anglers, whom I knew to be rude and uncouth, said you were ugly, that Sir Francis had been at it, that you were a throwback, Henrietta, unable to survive a winter in the wild. They said you displayed plain, domestic qualities and, if Sir Francis was not responsible for fertilising the egg from which you hatched, some unscrupulous joker had slid a Sainsbury's domestic duck egg beneath your unsuspecting mother.

I cared not one jot what other people thought Henrietta, my love at first sight.

Henrietta, you grew into *my* ugly duckling, all tufty with new feathers and down. Then one Saturday, fully fledged, your beauty bursting through, you greeted me with a spread of your wings and fluttered from the water to my side. Henrietta, moving across the stony ground, sounding your approach, gliding to greet me with your waddling gait, you picked your passage gingerly and more gracefully than any damsel ever did on the catwalks of Paris.

Some Saturdays, before my maggoty hook had dipped into the water, you were by my side, billing at my boots, tugging on my worm-like laces. Cheekily, you would prize the lid from my maggot box and gobble up many a writhing beak-full. Checking bait quality, like some fussy housewife, you were well set in your ways. Henrietta, your name I chose the first time you visited me; a beautiful name, it popped into my head in a solitary moment of inspired creation: a name unique to you, which I would never shorten. You were Henrietta the duck, the duck I loved.

Sir Francis often tried to muscle in, to move you on, Henrietta, to demand loudly he have authority over you. We repulsed him. That deftly directed kick, I planted beneath his tail, sent him skedaddling across the pond, had him performing tantrums and gyrations, such was his paddy. Henrietta, there was room for no one else in our lives.

During an autumn squall, rain deluged, thunder roared overhead, lightning split an adjacent tree asunder, sending disused crow nests flying. Alarmed, Henrietta, you leapt into my lap, buried your body deep beneath my waterproofs. Squirming in, you turned around, poked your head out and there you stayed. Perhaps you felt my warmth, flutters from my heart, our spirits communing, or you had found a safe repose. Whichever it was, Henrietta, you chose that sanctuary each Saturday thereafter, as the first of that winter's frosts and its northerly winds chilled the ground and edged the pond with frills of ice.

Winter was upon us that Saturday. Fishing for the year was ending. Late afternoon, I launched you gently away from me onto the pond. I watched you paddle off, unsure if I would ever see you again. Then you surprised me. You turned. Bustling from the water, you were intent on forsaking your world for mine. My basket was open; you fluttered up and clambered into it.

I recall dusk had fallen and, suddenly, in the distance, I heard the sound of shotguns announcing the presence of poachers. The sky had darkened further: birds were whirling overhead, panic stricken, unsure of their safety.

You were calm, Henrietta. I took you home to a safe haven.

Day after day, nestling by the fire, your head beneath your wing, you watched me with a loving eye. You shared my house, my life, for one whole, long, freezing winter

Occasionally though, during the long winter months and when the weather was fine, I took you back to the pond. For your happiness,

I hoped that you might return to the wild; alas, wild duck hormones dormant, you always returned with me, Henrietta: we were one.

Then I killed you Henrietta.

Spring was almost upon us again that lovely, sunny Saturday. 'What a lovely day it is for a paddle,' I said to you over breakfast as you gobbled up your mealworms. You agreed. At noon, we set out for the pond.

I had forgotten Sir Francis. When you, filled with delight, plunged into the water, he paddled up to you, fussed around you noisily, bullying you away from me. Nudging you like a tug against an ocean liner, he pushed you out into deeper water, way beyond my reach. I felt your concern. I heard it in your voice.

Henrietta, you often soared into the sky, he in your wake. Wheeling sharply, you tried to escape his clutches, but he always gained the upper hand. When you splashed down, he kept himself between us. I panicked as dusk descended. I was fearful of the night's menaces and the treachery of Sir Francis.

As the evening star winked into life, I stood alone in the twilight. The moon, rising and lying just above the land, cast a wan light over the pond, sending spiky shadows streaking. Once more, I saw your whiteness loft into the night and then your silhouette, black against the moon, with Sir Francis, your pernickety escort, closely attending.

The whapping of your wings receded as you winged towards the copse. Neither you nor I realised you were winging into danger. Suddenly, flashes lit up the sky, shotguns sounded, booming and echoing. I read deadly omens in those dreadful reports. Birds filled the sky in confusion and you were airborne, a splendid poacher's target set against the backdrop of the rising moon. That you had filled their sights numbed my thoughts.

The clamour abated suddenly. Birds had struck out for safer feeding grounds and for one solitary moment, the night was still.

The gunshots had stunned my hearing Henrietta. Your laboured approach went unheard. Your injured, pained body in flight, your love giving you strength to reach me on the shore went unseen. Then I felt the rush of air, the feather-light kiss brushing my face, your dead body, violated by poachers' pellets, whizzing past my head Henrietta, to strike the ground at my feet with a sickening whump.

I picked you up Henrietta, cradled you in my arms, held your floppy neck, looked into your dulled eyes, tried to wipe blood from your feathers with my tears. Vainly, I sought signs of life.

Distraught, I cried out to the moon, 'Come back to me Henrietta, I beseech you,' words I had wrung from my besotted, sorrowing heart. Henrietta, I was begging you to return and break the chains that would bind me in purgatory, from where I could never escape.

The rustling of undergrowth disturbed my mournful sloth. Bulky figures, game bags stuffed with poachers' fare, pushed through briar and thorn. I stood still in their midst, shell-shocked, seemingly a source of amusement. Then, Henrietta, a voice, gruff and countrified said the mind changing words that, on reflection, whetted my appetite for you, Henrietta 'Would Henry prefer his duck crispy or with noodles.'

Henrietta, you have arrived. I see the Chinese chef has caressed your plucked and gutted body with fine oils infused with oriental spices. Cooked gently to that poacher's suggestions, crispy on the restaurant's spit, your skin is now of the reddish hue ensuring the wonderful, succulent finish that I will relish. Henrietta, you look so appetising, so tempting on the sizzling platter, your hissing juices releasing final aromatised reminders of your wildness.

Henrietta, you had a surprising end, Cor, Love a Duck.

Jane's Dilemma Answered

As the door closed behind her, Jane put the letter that she'd found lying on the passage carpet into her handbag and guiltily looked up. She knew the letter would come, had thought long and hard on how to deal with its contents when it did, but had no ready answers. She was about to take the short walk to the corner shop to collect fresh milk and a newspaper. She'd use the walk to gather her thoughts.

The envelope had a Belgian stamp and an Antwerp postmark. It could only be only be from her husband, George, a merchant seaman. The 'Airmail' letter had a posting date stamp four days previously. The area around her heart tightened in pain and her stomach muscles tensed. Liverpool, the ship's homeport, was only two days away from Antwerp by sea. George could already have docked there and be on his way home!

George's letters, from his many foreign ports of call, had always contained a declaration of his undying love for her, and a promise (never kept) that he'd never go deep sea again. Then the telephone call would come from Liverpool, on his ship's arrival there. Over the phone and filled with excitement, George would re-declare his undying love; promise weeks of never ending sex during his leave, as it used to be. Jane had heard it many times before.

George's excuse for staying in the Merchant Navy was that the sea had a calling on men, him in particular, and she would never understand. Often she had thought no, her life couldn't go on like this: she needed her man at home. But it had taken time to stop kidding herself, realising eventually that it darned well wasn't the call of the sea at all; it was the attraction of having a girl in every port. That's what kept him away from her.

Which was why, twelve months previous, soon after George had sailed, a girl friend was able to encourage her to attend an over twenty-five's night at the local Locarno. 'It's a 'grab a granny night', you'll love it,' the friend said. And she did. There she had met Billy, a handsome, pleasant, divorced young man who was seeking companionship. Before long, they were an item and sleeping together regularly. What the hell, George was at it too, probably in every port of call he made and all over the world.

Then, when she became pregnant with Billy's baby, Billy took off, not wanting the responsibility.

As she re-entered the house the cry of her one-month-old baby son took her to the bedroom. She lifted the hungry child, transferring it to the pram in the kitchen. She changed the soiled nappie and took it out the back door, dumping it in the bin. She filled the electric kettle and switched it on. Put milk into the child's bottle, she put it into the microwave to warm.

She looked around for some other task to delay opening the letter, but there was nothing but a pile of ironing, which could wait. With her chest heaving, she removed the letter from her handbag. Nervously with a knife jerking in her hand she slit open the envelope. With trembling fingers, she removed a tawdry piece of writing paper and unfolded it. Fully opened she saw George's scrawl.

Dear Jane, Sorry to disappoint you but I have found another woman. I am asking for a divorce so that I can marry her, for she is expecting my baby. I will not be coming home again, but hope everything is okay with you. All the best,

George

A Whimsical View On How Political Correctness Influences Policing

Many Police Forces adopted the recruitment policy of encouraging graduate men and women into the Job. The dangled carrot was a course in etiquette, political correctness, man management and law at an Officer Training College, the guarantee of never having to walk a beat and a place on the nanolubricant-greased fast track to the higher echelons of a Force.

These Forces placed no restrictions on the recruitment of the vertically challenged, or those with a degree in Zoology being their only qualification. Some four-foot-four-inches tall recruits, with very long arms and lengthy, slender index fingers, had better qualifications and experience in small-animal midwifery than many vets.

Accordingly, detectives on these Forces' strengths worried about the impact the political correctness drive would have on their positions; they also believed their Guv'nors intensive efforts to improve educational standards would result in these unwelcome graduates taking the posts of the most experienced men and women in the ranks. It was becoming increasingly clear that guv'nors considered them dinosaurs, although there were successful thief takers and others with good policing skills and specialist abilities amongst detective ranks.

Cushy numbers weren't just jeopardised; they disappeared overnight! Reappointment to the front line wasn't threatened; it happened immediately! Some detectives considered the changes putting them back into uniform and back on the beat detrimental to their future happiness within their Force.

Gloom also infiltrated the minds of those still waiting the inevitable shunting from their detective rank. Despondency soared. The detectives involved in the shakeup perceived madness in political correctness. It ripped away their love of the Job and denied them the major perks normally enjoyed by plain-clothes officers.

Sir Robert Peel was the first senior copper to consider mumping a problem. However, beat bobbies of his time and today would not agree. They appreciated the cup of tea or a coffee offered in kitchens of cafes or private homes, the meals offered and consumed with lip-smacking relish once through the back door of oriental restaurants. Likewise, the discounts on purchases offered to beat bobbies whilst shopping off duty wearing their uniform shirt, collar and tie, they saw as an integral part of policing and welcome perks of the Job.

Today's guv'nors never condoned these practices, even though, as beat bobbies, they probably wholeheartedly indulged in the tradition. Bobbies found a brief dally off the regular beat to visit such a mumping hole for free refreshment, often resulted in some information being passed, which led to a noteworthy arrest.

Traditionally, as well as exploiting these mumping opportunities, detectives repaired to the pub at lunchtime there, over a pie and a pint, to fabricate enough evidence 'to put chummy away'. Experienced detectives knew that the clampdown on such activities was a political-correctness-inspired decision that jeopardised C.I.D successes in thousands of future prosecutions.

Some detectives, reappointed to the drudgery and foot-aching slog of beat duty, experienced deep upset, thought the change a demotion, an insult to their years of devoted service and left their Force in droves. The numbers volunteering to join the detective rank fell; being an undernourished detective with unsound or uncorroborated evidence to bring to the witness box was hardly an attractive career move.

The lot of detectives declined catastrophically, as had the uniformed strength's of all Forces, the reduction worrying Guv'nors and politicians alike. The opposition leader's loud rants rattled the rafters of the House of Commons during Prime Minister's Questions, bitterly laying blame at the door of the government of the day for not tackling the police numbers question with energy, urgency and wit.

A decision taken at the highest level decreed that numbers had to improve, the drain reversed. However, the days of the much-loved pie and pint culture, wearing the shopping shirt off duty and mumping were gone forever, consigned by the introduction of political correctness into the dustbin of Forces' histories, without hope of resurrection.

RIP the old-fashioned bobby and his lot.

The Return Of The Hunt

We had flagged on the steep climb, but gathered pace breasting the hill and again on taking to the slope leading down to the village. Our cottages, in the distance, black eaves desolate beneath their snow covering, offered welcoming hearths and blazing log fires with warmth to revitalise our extremities, albeit painfully.

The snow lay crisp, crunching beneath our blistered feet as we trudged. My huntsmen walked hunched, their reddened faces hidden inside fur-lined cowls. Breathing heavily, they left wisps of white hanging in the chill, afternoon air.

The hunt's successfulness encumbered the men; all carried rabbits, hares and pheasants, strung in pairs over shoulders. Gideon, my eldest son, my pride, was strong, doughty. He carried the prize stag on his back.

The dogs moved carefully at our sides. The tenderness in their bleeding paws the result of their chases over ground frozen, hard and sharp.

Helmut was my youngest son. That day his actions were weighty on my heart. On his eighteenth birthday, he lagged behind, out of sight… where he belonged.

The hunt had gathered at daybreak as the orange glow of a low sun kissed the clear sky of morning and lit the forbidding tops of icy crags far to the east. My huntsmen had already wiped the night's sleep from their eyes. Clapping their hands together and stamping their feet in unison, they were keeping warming blood flowing towards cold-sensitive fingertips and toes.

From the kennel the dogs had scampered joyously, quivering along the length of their bodies as they finished their ablutions; they knew the signs: they were about to hunt.

Well wrapped and ready, we set off at a steady pace towards the west and the forest. The icy air struck our faces like the nick from a well-honed razor; our nostrils were freezing up on each laboured inhalation.

The sun, lifting slowly, sent our spiky shadows streaking towards the glistening, frosted, forest topping ahead of us. Helmut led us across the snow plain, his stave testing the snow before each step, searching for hidden deepenings. It was his day. Today was his coming of age. But he looked back often towards the house; from the doorstep, his mother watched the departure of her cherished one.

Our passage was arduous; a stumbling procession until reaching the forest edge. The dogs followed, padding in our wake, sticking to the firmer, trampled snow. Walking was easier beneath the trees where only a sprinkling of snow had filtered through the thick foliage of the canopy of stark branches and pine needles cocooned in ice.

We circled the forest edge until we came down wind; there was a light breeze coming up the valley, but the sun had no strength to move it much. The dogs, obedient veterans of the hunt, jostled behind, quietly waiting their cue.

Droppings, recent and moist, lay on the light snow covering; this sign and two sets of hoof prints pointed to deer passing recently. The patch of nibbled bark on a tree and a branch stripped of its frozen needles, spoor that suggested we were on the same trail through the forest that the deer were taking.

Ahead, the wood thinned as it met the rise of the mountainside. It was a good place to find deer; more space existed there for the dogs to work their quarry. We stopped, listened in the silence of the forest. Only the occasional fluttering of snow dropping from the canopy disturbed the stillness. Moving cautiously forward, we heard the crack, the breaking of frozen branches. The dogs tucked in behind us, all of them adopting the pounce position. They knew the signs; knew the waiting game was ending.

As the dogs crept forward, each had their eyes straining, looking for some four-legged form beyond the jumble of briar, ferns and low branches. They all had cocked ears, tuned for the order, listening for the mad pounding of a fleeing animal's hooves, ready to spring in pursuit and dash in for the kill.

Cautiously, watching our footing, we flitted from tree to tree, our heads weaving, peering low for a view through the thinnest foliage.

Helmut was to the fore. On this day, his day, the first sighting of game was to be his privilege; he, too, would call the dogs to the chase. But he looked ill at ease in his task, shivering in his furs, his face pinched and cold, showing no excitement, no eagerness for involvement. The huntsmen and Gideon exchanged glances behind him such was their concern.

Suddenly, we came upon a parting in undergrowth. Two stags were scraping at the frozen ground in the clearing ahead. Helmut saw them too, I was sure, though he gave no indication of doing so.........but if he didn't react soon, they'd have our scents and their flight was certain.

I nudged Helmut, made eye contact and quietly signalled him to unleash the dogs with the one word they all understood... Kill.

Helmut's face betrayed his inner agony; it had tied his tongue.

Gideon, like me, was a born hunter. Sensing a problem, he took the initiative. One look from him and a quiet whisper of, 'Kill,' to the dogs was enough. At once, they were all in full flight, bursting through the low branches. The stags, briefly stunned by the crashing sound, flagged for danger, but too late. The dogs were on them swiftly; of the two, it was the older stag who took the force of the pack, the younger escaping, thrashing through brushwood and gorse to safety.

The old stag was down, kicking his last when we raced into the clearing. The lead dog's fangs had tightly locked around its windpipe. The entire pack had applied tooth, each tearing at its throat. In its death throes, the old stag wheezed, its tongue lolled and slavers sprayed. Then, with one, final rasping exhalation, its rolling, fear-bulged eyes stilled and it was dead.

I pulled my skinning knife from its sheath and ordered the dogs to stand back. As a father and hunt master I had a duty. Today in the forest that had fed our families for generations, I would blood my youngest son. I had initiated all my huntsmen with deer blood on their coming of age. With one hand, I took hold of the stag's scut, hacking it off close to the rump with the knife. The main artery in the neck I sliced open and wet the scut in the weeping blood.

Helmut looked on, his eyes wide, his face turned deathly white. He knew the ritual of the blooding: the gentle daub on the forehead with the warm ooze, but showed reluctance to participate in this ancient ceremony. As I walked proudly towards him, blood dripping from scut to snow, leaving behind a trail of crimson droplets, I saw his face twitching, and the bead of sweat glistening on his forehead in the chill of the morning. He took several steps backwards first, then turned away from me. His lips parted and the thin gruel of his breakfast spewed onto the snow in a yellowy arc. Leaning over moaning, he cleared his throat, spitting out a gob. As he straightened and caught my concerned, narrowed eyes, his body began shaking. Throwing a hand to his forehead, he turned away from me and raced away to seek solitude in the darkness of the forest.

I stood alone, downcast that my son should turn away from me on his confirmation of manhood. Gideon moved forward and put an arm around my shoulders. 'He is but a raw youth and not yet ready for such manly pursuits. He'll change, given time,' he commiserated.

Gideon's face was as square and as solid as his dependability, his eyes brown, deep, as were my father's and mine. Helmut's face was long, his eyes blue. I recognised his mother's much softer looks and her kind nature in him. Perhaps it was only time that stood between him and the acceptance of killing to eat and the traditions of the hunt.

Custom dictated, too, that the hunter and his blooded son led the returning hunt into the village. There, all would rejoice at the return of the man who had left that morning a boy. Sighting the stag on Gideon's shoulders, the villagers expected to hear of Helmut's initiation.

Even from the distance, I recognised all who thronged at the foot of the slope. All had left their work or their play to congratulate Helmut. When their cheering began, I pulled my furry cowl forward to hide my face.

Suddenly, I heard the crunch of snow as long, purposeful strides brought a figure from the rear to join me at my right hand. I glanced to my side. It was Helmut. He was carrying the bloodied scut that I'd thrown after his fleeing figure as it departed the clearing to skulk out of sight, in darkness. Now I saw running down his face, less troubled now but turned pink, a streak of dark blood from the daub congealing on his forehead.

Helmut smiled at me and put his arms about me. Pulling me tight towards him, he said quietly, 'I am with you, father.'

My head rose, my shoulders pulled back and, with the tear I shed soon to freeze over, I breathed out a greater white cloud. It was as men Helmut and I walked together, heads held high, proudly into the village

The Joys Of Greyhound Ownership

Paddy kept the greyhounds in a shed, surrounded by a high, fenced run, in the yard at the back of the cottage. On Friday nights, race nights in Dublin, feeding them came later. Within the house, a pan bubbled on the kitchen cooker; the skinned sheep's head grinning out surrounded by dancing onions, carrots, and spuds. Meat fell off the bone, eyes hung out from their sockets, boiled brains burst through the hole left by the slaughterman's cleaver. An overpowering smell of mutton dripping rose from the pot.

Paddy, his face red and windblown from bricklaying all day in the cold air of the building site, was sitting down at the corner table in the kitchen, ready to tuck in to his dinner. He was still wearing his working overalls. Molly his wife was sitting opposite him, glaring at him, neat in her starched pinafore. 'Aren't you going to change out of your working gear before eating?' she erupted.

Paddy shook his head. 'Tonight, working gear's my official greyhound-handling outfit at the track, as far as I'm concerned. I wouldn't want to be looking too successful at the track. My appearance might keep the odds up. The bookies there give short odds if they think your dog's got a chance.'

The other item of his working attire, the donkey jacket, spattered with cement and mud, with 'Murphy's the Builders' written on the back, hung over his chair. He pulled his plate closer to him and plunged a fork into the pile of corned beef hash plastered next to the colcannon and chips on his plate. As he ate, he occasionally lifted the fag sitting on a saucer close by and took a drag from it.

Molly was broader in the shoulders than he was. That made her the boss… in her eyes anyway. Beneath the table, she had begun to run a slippered foot up and down Paddy's leg. Friday nights usually promised a little romance later, when he got home from the track and had fed and settled the dogs. But she'd have to keep his mind on it and enquired hopefully, 'You won't be having your usual bellyful of Guinness before you get home tonight?'

Occasionally Paddy stayed off the booze on Fridays, retaining enough energy after his week's labour to be of use to her in bed. With a little early prompting, she'd hope of steering his thoughts towards the promise, and he'd be without the rasping, beery, laboured breath she had often suffered.

Looking at Paddy busily eating, she grimaced. She could see his romantic thoughts were as far gone as the sheep's, whose head was being boiled to useless bone in the pot. To him, that night's racing; how his dogs might run and how much he'd wager on them were more important. The gurgling pan spat broth in their direction while they ate the meal, which was less nourishing than the dog's was.

Paddy, his thinking complete, blew out some smoke, put the fag down on a saucer and said. 'The dogs are fit, keen, and well handicapped. I think they'll both win their races tonight and I'll have a good bet on them.'

Molly waved one hand at the smoke, squirted tomato sauce onto her plate with the other, and replied, asserting her place in the dog's training schedule. 'They're only fit because it's I that walks them. You only take them down to the pub to brag with your cronies over their fitness, buy them crisps, have them laying about in the fag ash, the slops, and the spittle.'

Paddy had always feigned shortage of time and tiredness after work for him to walk the dogs, conceding superior greyhound training techniques to Molly, when it suited him. Molly, he knew, enjoyed the thought of being superior to him in that regard. But Paddy was always up for a bit of teasing. 'Now, now,' he said, rapping the bottom of the salt cellar onto the table, then prodding at the pourer hole with a prong of his fork, 'it's more than walks that makes a dog fit. Look at that sheep's head now, its brains melting into strength-giving succulent gravy.

'Tis full o' proteins and vitamins that pot is. Tis the real McCoy, to be sure. Many a dog owner'd like to know the secret of my dog's diet. Track record grub it is. Make them fizz around the track, it will.'

Molly had to get her greyhound racing knowledge heard. 'If Sean from the slaughterhouse wasn't my cousin, you'd never have got hold of sheeps' heads. They're rarely available these days. It was him that told you about the old ways of feeding the dogs for winning. 'None of that sterile bagged shite... none of that Wuffitmix,' he told you. 'Get the sheep's head fired into them along with some veg and stale brown-bread,' he said. That and me walking them, that's what's winning the races. It's all down to that.'

Molly withdrew her slippered foot fully expecting a kick, wolfed down a fork of food, then returned her attention to Paddy... 'Feck all to do with you, it is.'

'Ach Molly, away with yer, you're having yourself on if you think it's all down to you. Tis it not myself what takes the dogs over the farmer's fields, slips them after a rabbit, keeps them spry and keen enough to go after the dummy hare? And to be sure is it not myself what guts the rabbits then feeds them raw to the dogs...?'

Molly sniffed loudly, interrupting Paddy whilst he was in full flow. 'You never take them out often enough. More often, the howls of them wanting walking sounds like Dublin Central Police Station cells on a Saturday night... And don't come close to me again with yer stinking fingers after the gutting.'

'...And I'm always rubbing the dogs down after the races and taking them for short cooling off walks. Tis my fingers that gets into their muscles, kneads them, makes sure they lie at night easy in their beds and get up in the morning without the stiffness created by the mad dash of the race?'

Molly got up, splashed her plate in the sink, swirled her hand around in the water, as if in emphasis, and turned, saying. 'And don't come near me after you've been rubbing down the dogs with that stuff. I smelled like an asthmatic's chest after you'd been pawing at me.'

'Dog's liniment's strong stuff,' said Paddy, and finished his supper with a crash of utensils, 'goes for my eyes, too, it does.'

'Owners should do it for their dogs without complaint... if they cared,' Molly fired back at him.

'I never complain. I love my dogs,' Paddy quickly got in.

Molly saw Paddy was reacting to her carping, even though his eyes were staring into the fag smoke as she removed his plate. 'Caring owners walk their dogs too. 'Five miles a day,' cousin Sean told you was the proper distance. But that's too much like hard work for you, Paddy. Puffing too much at the auld fags, spitting and coughing up yellow phlegm, keeping me awake all night with your barking...'

'Ach woman, give me a break.'

'... Worse than the dogs, you are. One of these days, a coughing bout'll break your back in two places you silly auld fool. Aye...leave the graft to daft Molly.'

Paddy was enjoying the craik, seeing Molly get uppity. He'd try some more, make her blazing in bed later. 'It's woman's work keeping them clean, shovelling up the shite from the yard, and walking them while I'm out at work during the day to be sure and...'

'Keeping them clean? Keeping them clean?' Molly interjected. 'When was the last time you put your shoulder to a brush and did any cleaning? There's sometimes more shite out there than came out of Paisley's jaws.'

'...I was going to say I'd put a fiver on the nose for you tonight because you deserve it. To buy yourself a new dress, but seeing as you think you know better than me you can put yer own fiver on.'

'A fiver on, do you say. When did I ever have a fiver to put on anything?

'You get all me wages.'

'Except your drink and fag money.'

'A man needs a fag and a drink after a hard day on the site, woman.'

'You're drunk too often.'

'No wonder when the likes of you are always nagging.'

'Get going and get back here for your shower. The dogs will be climbing the fencing. They know it's Friday night too... you know?

The two dogs had laid in the dark since Paddy arrived home from work, their eyes never leaving the back door of the cottage. Grub could be coming through that door in a bowl or Paddy with the leads to take them walking or racing. Either way, they were on a hair-trigger to leap into life.

Paddy stood up from the table and hoisted the donkey jacket over his shoulders. It smelled warm; the results of a day's graft had not disappeared. He stubbed his cigarette out, pushed in and rattled his chair against the table, turned quickly and took the leads from the hook behind the back door. He left the cottage leaving the back door open behind him; the presence of greyhounds in the kitchen leaping around looking for grub got Molly's dander up as well.

The two dogs streaked from the shed, vying for position. Both stretched their bodies out, yelping in excitement, then leapt at the fencing in the greeting Paddy expected. He had the gate just ajar when the dogs pushed past him, knocking him aside, their minds on the kitchen. Grub was always more important when nothing resembling a hare moved.

At the sink, Molly heard the padding paws mount the step, the paws landing and sliding on the floor covering, and one dog squeal as it collided with the table. Then she felt the paws clamber up her back, and the cold noses snuffling their greetings around her neck before she could turn. Quickly they were gone, paws up on the table looking for scraps, noses in the butter dish. Then she saw them sniffing over the top of the pot, only the heat dissuading further interest.

Paddy appeared at the door, a smile splitting his face and called for the dogs to come. Then to Molly, 'They love you just as much as me, to be sure.'

Molly began figuring out the meaning of Paddy's words, while gingerly removing the pinafore with the dogs' paw marks in smelly brown newly imprinted on it.

Heavy Rock Artist Aged 10 1/2

When the fine, big house burned to the ground, the owners left it a charred ruin, too dangerous to enter. We waited until the bulldozers knocked it down and workers dumped the debris on the tip behind the council houses. Only then did we begin rummaging for anything useful.

The tip was our natural playground. We had more fun there than sitting watching black and white telly. The fire had charred most of the stuff, but there was recoverable wood from the upper floors, wall linings and roof. While it lasted, we made a few bob cutting it into bundles, selling it to the wifies around the doors.

Being ten and a half, I suppose I was the ringleader. My two chums, Jimmy and Tommy, were a full, useful year younger than I was. They were always looking up to me. I was the bright one, see, the one with all the good ideas, the one with business expertise enough to supplement their pocket money.

Tommy was the quiet, industrious one who selected the best wood to go under the saw and axe. Jimmy and I helped, but we'd begun to spend time taunting each other over the piano.

The grand piano, the likes of which I'd only seen in movies, its legs burnt to stumps, caused the stir. Although its keys had melted, congealed into a massive liquorice allsort; the day we found it dumped, I told Jimmy I'd get a tune out of it, before it ended up as kindling. Jimmy sniggered. 'You're talking rubbish. You'll never get a tune out of that.' His remarks stung me, got me going. I'd seen him messing about with it, pull a broken string taut, twang it, then try strumming it using a piece of twisted plastic from a white key, as if he was some Jimmy Hendricks.

I returned the snigger when all he got out of it was a dull whir.

Now, Jimmy awaited my performance and watched me circling the piano, peering into it, looking to see if any of its guts might still be working. He acted casual, looked a clever clogs in the wee workman's overalls that his mum always insisted he wore after school. In his hands were rolling tobacco and a Rizla paper. He had nicked the makings from his elder brother's baccy tin. Expertly he fashioned a thin cigarette without looking at it, licking along the sticky edge, acting the mature cowboy he had seen in Westerns.

The piano's innards lay twisted. Workmen dragging it from the house with machinery and little respect had broken the string tensioner. The hammers would never strike another note. Jimmy's eyes searched the skies as if he knew there wasn't a sound left in it.

Something had to leap into my thoughts, if I were to retain the useful edge of age and prove my innovation abilities to him.

The boulder we had used to smash difficult pieces of timber caught my eye. I sauntered towards it and forced it out of its muddy hole with the toe of my wellie. It was heavy, covered in mud, and I booted it towards the piano not knowing exactly what I'd do with it. I stooped and picked it up, balanced it on my chest, stepped onto remains of the keyboard, then onto a corner of the main frame, my feet resting on two wooden struts. Balancing was tricky and I rocked as I lifted the boulder to arm's length. I'd decided to smash it into the piano's guts and just shout out. 'Boom, boom.' It was all I could think of until my sudden rocking motion put the words into my head, 'Watch this Jimmy, and get ready to rock,' I shouted.

The piano had always lain at a slight angle. And when I had the boulder grasped in both hands above my head, I felt the piano shudder as it slipped sideways. The remaining stump of a leg had broken off. I overbalanced and my right foot slipped into the jumble of strings and other twisted pieces. My left leg, supporting the unbalanced weight, gave way, the boulder jettisoning from my grasp, over my head. Instead of following me down into the piano's guts, its descent was towards Jimmy, head down, and coughing from inhaling cigarette smoke.

I screamed, 'Jimmeeeee.'… My voice seemed to echo from the backs of houses. The boulder seemed motionless; we fell together, the rock brushing the tip of Jimmy's nose. Before Jimmy slumped motionless onto the ground, I saw blood spurting from his nostrils.

Tommy had heard my scream and by the time I'd clawed my way out of the piano, he was leaning over Jimmy's prone body and calling out, ' Jimmy, Jimmy, wake up,' and tapping him on the face with the flat of his hand.

Both of my knees and one elbow were grazed and bleeding, but I never noticed at the time. I joined Tommy and looked down at Jimmy's blood-spattered face. He was groaning, his eyes roving. Tommy took a dirty hanky from his pocket and pressed it to Jimmy's nose. Jimmy snatched at it, hollered in more pain. It was nothing sensible, but I picked out, 'Mum.'

Tommy looked at me terrified, then he sped off towards Jimmy's house, which was down the tip banking. I was petrified thinking of the belting I'd get for stupidly causing Jimmy's injury, thinking I'd broken his nose.

Jimmy's eyes began to focus. He rubbed them and sat up. Looking around, he said. 'Hide the fag before my mum gets here.' At least he was thinking straight and could hear.

I saw the curl of smoke rising behind Jimmy. 'You okay now?' I asked, whilst walking over to the fag. 'There's still a drag or two left in this,' I said, handing it to him.

'Throw it away. My Mum'll kill me if she catches me,' he mumbled.

'She'll kill me when she sees what I've done to your nose.' A blob of congealing blood hung from one nostril.

'We don't want to be stopped playing here and making a few bob. Don't want any hassle,' he said, getting to his feet now and swiping his hands at the mud clinging to his overalls.

His mum bustled up the bank, Tommy running by her side as she made her way around the piles of wood. I wondered what he had told her. Had he dropped me into the mire?

'Jimmeeeee…what have you been up to?' she shouted from a distance.

'Nothing, Mum,' he called towards her.

'I can't leave you boys playing together for a minute.' Words we'd heard so many times before.

'However did you manage to do that?' she cried. She was close to Jimmy, holding his shoulders, peering at his face. She took a clean tissue from her pinafore, wet it on her tongue, and dabbed at the dried blood under his nose and on his top lip.

Tommy held a finger across his lips. It was his sign for us to say nothing. Obviously, he hadn't told her what happened.

Jimmy said, 'I tripped and fell, Mum, it's nothing to worry about.'

'You'll be the death of me yet, frightening me like this,' she said, and sounded as if she meant it.

Jimmy's mum ambled off, chuntering. Together we laid into the piano, getting a tune from it with our axes and, before nightfall, it was broken into kindling worth five bob of any wifie's money.

Scouse Meets A Genie

A genie appears to a Liverpool FC supporter whilst he's walking his mongrel, late one night, behind the Liver Building, near the Pier head.

'I can give you one wish,' said the genie, 'what will it be?' he asked

Scouse said, 'I find it totally embarrassing. It's making me the laughing stock in Liverpool's Kop End on Saturdays. This dog of mine, known as Bobby since it was a pup, won't answer to any name now other than Roberto. It has also developed a phobia for the colour blue, and I'd like to be quickly rid of both the humiliating situations it's caused me.

'I cannot drag the stupid mutt from the house unless it is wearing its blue coat with the Everton Logo emblazoned thereon, blue collar and lead, and silly me with my pockets stuffed with toffees, which I have to feed to him regularly because he likes them.

'Roberto has only one leg the correct length, half a tail, no ears and is cross-eyed, all from fighting. He has one testicle missing. A mad beagle bitch savaged and chewed it off during a ferocious scrap.

'I would also like to see these defective or missing items replaced, Roberto reinvented as Bobby and titivated up, given a pedigree so I can enter him in Crufts.'

The genie said, 'You're asking too much. I'm not a miracle worker like Sir Alex Ferguson. Make another wish.'

Scouse asks, 'Can you make my beloved football team Liverpool good enough to qualify for the Champions League next season?'

The genie replied, 'I think I'd better take another look at Roberto!'

Carlisle United V Brighton & Hove Albion

A Game From The Past

Foxes Versus Seagulls: An Alternative Report

From the moment the Seagulls took to the pitch, in their Canary coloured strip, it seemed painful obvious to the loyal Foxes' supporters that they would have plenty about which to Grouse.

The pitch was bone hard from the overnight frost and an icy gale blew down its length from the Warwick Road end. Referee Hal Finch and his two linesmen, Ivor Ruff and Jack Daw, arrived late due to problems on the rail network, which delayed the kickoff by five minutes.

The Seagulls won the toss and chose to play with the wind at their backs, in an early attempt to capitalise on its assistance. Kicking towards the waterworks end, they faced their own supporters, who were perched high on the east terracing and heavily bedecked in the gaudy bunting of their calling.

From the first whistle, the Seagulls flew at the Foxes with devastating pace, leaving defenders floundering in their wake. Jacobs, enjoying an early little stint on the wing, received a well-directed cross ball and skilfully rounded Dave Rushberry, on the bounce. He then proceeded to tie Jack Ashurst in a knot before selling Don O'Riordan a stupendous dummy, leaving him in a state of utter bemusement and in some discomfort with a wryneck.

On reaching the dead-ball line, he swept over an inch perfect pass into the poorly defended box, to find Amos Connor in acres of space. Connor collected the ball on the volley and hit a dipper, which swerved swift and sure, low down into the right hand corner of Dave McKellar's goal.

McKellar, who had conceded more goals this season than in the whole of the last, remonstrated volubly with his pedestrian defence.

He had found their early season form hard to swallow, which had left him with a sore and infected whitethroat.

Referee Finch blew on his warbler for the goal, which sent the seagulls fans raving with delight. Flags waved as they jostled and jumped in a cacophony of delight, for indeed they had something to crow about

The seagulls' team, too, were in a rapturous mood, as they kissed and hugged. Doing the turkey trot hack to the middle, Foxes' supporters wished for the spread of millions of thrush germs amongst them, whilst celebrating their excellent good fortune, to be one up against this good, sturdy team from these northern climes.

From the restart, it was the Foxes applying the pressure to the Seagull's defence. Poskett, who must have been thinking it was too great a wrench for teams to rook the Foxes out of so many results recently, and to be one down, smacked a shot from the edge of the penalty area with superhuman ferocity. It hit the left hand post, making it rock like a stilt, only for the ball to rebound a tremendous distance up field, into the Foxes half. Standing there, on side, was Amos Connor, the scourge of the Foxes' defence. Taking the ball skilfully onto his pigeon chest, he knocked it down to his hen toes and turned like only Pele can, to race into the undefended goal area. He reached the box unchallenged and hit a roller. McKeller came out and although he was a bit of a fly catcher by hobby, he had no chance. Conner struck the ball sweetly into the back of the net and the result seemed goosed for the Foxes.

Two up, the Seagulls went wild as they ritualistically pecked each other on the cheek: an incautious celebration, thought the foxes' supporters.

Meanwhile, amongst the ranks of the meagre but loyal Foxes' support, faces of stone chatted together. Amongst them was the President of the Ladies' Supporters Club, Mag Pie, together with her turtle dove, Robin. Having supped many cans of Kestrel Lager, they gave bitter vent to their spleens and cawed taunts of a racialist nature at a certain celebrating great bustard that had just flown up the wing. They believed, no doubt, that Connor spending his next night in gale force winds high in a tree ample reward for the goal.

The referee blew for the end of the half, which had contained little hope for the home support. They were, however, entertained during the interval by the sight of the local Constabulary attempting to apprehend a mongrel, of part ridgeback descent, who answered to Lewis and who had strayed onto the pitch, obviously on the hunt for some field fare. He was eventually cornered, collared and handed over to his owner after an announcement requested him to collect his cur Lew.

Mr Hal Finch, president for life of the Brighton and Hove Royal Society for the Protection of Birds, blew for the start of the second half. The Foxes, beginning the half at a two goal disadvantage, now had the wind at their backs to assist them in their comeback efforts.

From the kick off, Don O 'Riordan, who had been enjoying his role of covering in defence and supporting the attack, received instructions from the manager at the interval to wax wing-ward more often. This he had done and the ploy worked almost immediately when, on the hour, he received the delightfully weighted cross Bill Bishop sent over from the centre circle, out to the left.

Dribbling with great skill, he craftily attracted their right back Hutchings from his position on the corner of the box. He showed him the ball for one tantalising moment, but Hutchings committed a booby, bought the dummy and O'Riordan was past him. Leaving Hutchings to mourn and quail at his passing, and with his bald pate glistening with sweat in the glow of the floodlights, he raced onwards. Homing in on goal, O'Riordan placed his shot diagonally across the Keeper, drilling the ball past him, leaving him flat footed, for he was no diver, to hit the far post and rebound into the net.

Now it was the Foxes turn to rejoice. The strains of 'Do you ken John Peel' drifted from the directors ' box, being eager to encourage the players and were, themselves, ravenous for success.

The last twenty minutes of the game was a period of to-ing and fro-ing, during which neither side put themselves into a position from which they could create chances. Then, as the minutes ticked away and the Foxes despaired for an equaliser, fate cruelly took the game from their grasp.

A throw in half way into the Foxes' half, Penney optimistically headed on. It landed in a position of no great danger, just inside the box, where Jackie Ashurst, having one of his usual industrious games, went to clear. He smacked the ball with some venom and cleared it to safety up the park. Within the penalty area, however, little Alan Shoulder had been having a Jostle with Kraal during which he pulled his shirt for a lark. Mac Casa, the substitute linesman had noticed the foul and drew the referee's attention to it. Foxes' supporters thought this a rough decision as referee had co-opted the new assistant from the ranks of seagull supporters, following the injury to Ivor Ruff, which made it impossible for him to proceed.

After lengthy consultations between the two officials, the referee awarded a penalty. The Foxes thought this was a bit of tough justice and skulked around the referee. He was unmoved by their histrionic yapping and calmly blew the whistle to allow Hamish Wilson to drill home the Killer blow from the spot.

As the game teetered to its final, inevitable conclusion, both as a result and as a spectacle, the loyal supporters began to make their way home, a sure sign of the mounting frustration in the hearts of both themselves and the slowing players.

Many of the faithful, who had witnessed the slump in form of United, may ruefully reflect on Shoulder's brush with Kraal as the turning point of the match. However, it was plain to the knowledgeable that, although the players had warmed to the task of winning at home, both collectively and individually, they had been devoid of native cunning. It would have been the same result had they attempted a hundred shots at goal, for the ball would just not flamin' go into the net for them.

Hawkeye The Noo

The Progression Of A Mischievous Boy

Through The Development Of A Humorous Mind, Then To Stringing Words Together, Hoping Readers Find Them Funny In Print.

Growing up in the small hamlet of Ruthwell, Dumfriesshire, in the 1940s, villagers had reason to name me 'that white-headed boy, the worst boy in the village'. Obviously, they saw in me a mischievous, boyish mind; there are few of those residents left today, to see its development into off-the-wall humorous.

Certainly, I got into some scrapes: ringing the church bell on a Sunday afternoon, comes to mind. A classmate grassed me to the schoolmaster; next morning, he gave me six of the belt. Another set of sore hands I received for putting the school clock forward ten minutes, allowing students to leave early.

I'm quite white headed again these days: little has changed!

Recently, I did stand-up comedy in my daughter's pub, as 'That Little Rascal', earning £125 in donations for The Nicola Murray Foundation, the ovarian cancer charity that now receives donations from all my book sales.

In 1961, as a 21-year-old, I went to sea as an electrician, in the British Merchant Navy, with the Shaw Savill Line (now defunct). In those days, seafarers relied, mainly, for entertainment, whilst away from land, from the BBC Overseas Service. Often this was listening to fades, howls, whistles, static and crackling reception, hoping to hear something understandable and from home breaking through the ether.

Indeed, to survive, in the 'Merch', in those days, one had to have a thick skin; be able to withstand the daily Mickey-taking and windups that old-seadog shipmates resorted to, attempting to create amusement. Of course, if you could give back as good as you got, as I

48

did, you became proficient in the art, standing alongside the best exponents and learning from them. Of the six first-trippers that trip, four of us were Jocks; those skilled, pisstake aficionados had pots of targets to shoot at.

I married my sweetheart, Patricia, in Hull in 1964. She died in March 2014 of ovarian cancer. We were eight days short of our golden wedding celebration. Since her diagnosis in December 2010, my books have raised more than £2500 for ovarian cancer charities.

My efforts in helping to raise funds to find an ovarian cancer cure might not save a woman's life, but if they spotlight the dangers of ignoring symptoms of the disease, that early diagnosis is essential, and if one woman takes notice and asks for a referral to a cancer specialist, I will be happy.

In 1965, I became a Metropolitan Policeman. My writing then was only in police report books, in the prescribed manner, a sergeant's glower promised if you penned something in a humorous style. However, old timers passed on police lore, the humorous chestnuts that abounded, some I have used in my Jock Connection on the trail of Billy Bagman the Colostomy Comic book, just to forward the story. Hello, hello, what do we have here, I did not use.

In 1967, I returned to seafaring, remaining in that career until retirement, with lower-back problems, in 1989. My current writing is The Irking of Rupert Sewell, about a purser who finds work on a ferry running between UK and The Irish Republic. I ended my seagoing career on P&O ferries, on their Irish service, and have an inkling of what a purser, new to Irish ways and humour, might find irksome.

Only when a friend's wife said, 'You have the ability to string together words and make them sound funny,' did I consider attempting a novel; luckily, the Godsend of the word processor made writing for the untrained typist that much easier.

My literary heroes in those early days were Spike Milligan and Tom Sharpe. Milligan's Puckoon and Sharpe's Ancestral Vices I read more than once.

I love the silliness of Irish humour. The Jock Connection book concludes in a fictitious Irish Quarter, in East London, known to coppers as the I.Q. Indeed, you will find daftness there as well as cunning.

Where else would you find a character named Morphy O'Richards, who didn't know if his mammy named him after the kitchen toaster or somebody with an atrocious Irish accent? Where else would you find a Cream tribute band, all members transvestites, called Milk on the Turn? Or a hermaphrodite goat with both pendulous udder and testicles, led by a potty police sergeant. Or tales of Grampy O'Sullivan, who had won the Navigator's Den pub liar of the year contest for 57 years, consecutively. How Granny O'Sullivan instructed Grampy, if winning the final time, as expected, he should accept the divan suite prize, only for him to return home trundling a diving suit in a wheelbarrow.

Then there's the community police officer of twenty-five years, Constable William Beckham, who never had an arrest to make. Could he be moonlighting as Billy Bagman the Colostomy Comic, you might ask? Is he gigging in the I.Q.? That's what the Jock Connection are coerced into finding out.

I wrote most of the gags the comic tells.

The senior police officers, I give a hard time, in many ways, including painful lover's nuts for one.

The life of Riley and his 'troubles' book is set in Northern Ireland, in fictitious County Boil, where we find the town of Ballyboil nestling beneath the rolling foothills of the twin, carbuncular peaks of Mount Boil, the River Boil, formed from the tributary known as the Simmer Burn, meandering through the town. The town has a badass biker gang known as the Unlanced Boils; the town's police sergeant is intent on squeezing their heads. Ouch!

The journey begins in Belfast when recruit to an armed Republican outfit, Mickey O'Rourke, accidently murders the commander, Martin Muldoony, then flees the 'heavies' who want revenge.

The story then shifts to the shenanigans of the unfaithful Doctor Dernehen.

The doctor's wife, Dotty, is hot on the scent of her finagling husband. She suspects him of having an affair, and intends to catch him on the job, literally. In the end, it all turns out nastily for the sergeant, the doctor reprieved, until, with luck, good health and recharged imagination, I resurrect him in another book.

The blessing of publishers like Autharium has allowed unknown, unsigned writers to have their work advertised and sold on the internet. The process avoids submitting manuscripts to literary agents and publishers, the anxious wait and the ensuing rejection slips for all but the lucky. I know a published writer whose work publishers rejected nine times. He resubmitted to the first publisher approached and had his work accepted. Such hurdles would dishearten most writers to persist along that route.

However, most writers will still consider a publishing deal the Holy Grail. At my age, I'm just happy to have discovered Matt Bradbeer's Autharium. If, this winter, I persist with my third humorous novel, I will not look past online publishing, even if the returns remain skinny. The removal of VAT on downloads, made par with books, by the chancellor, will make online publishing much more worthwhile. Apparently, it's something in the EU that prevents its removal.

The printer of my self-published paperbacks started school on the same day as me and still runs his print company. He does me a decent price for my books, even when the runs are for 25 of each book. He realises that I make no personal profit, donating all I earn from the paperbacks to an ovarian cancer charity. I could have thousands printed for a smaller price per book, but I'm not vain enough and my garage floor would sag beneath the weight.

Long live Amazon the new publisher of my paperback and digital books.

Calling Back

The word 'back' has had a meaningful place in my life. Back it has in yours, too. There are things that I know nothing of, but back then, and it makes sense, if my father had gone back to the chemists for another packet of condoms, then I might not be here at all.

My Grandfather brought the family back to Scotland, back home. If he'd put the move on the backburner, I could be back living in Cardiff. He moved the family to his old backyard, fearing Hitler having a backlash at Cardiff. Had someone given the monster backchat?

Back in his old stamping ground, my Grandfather took up backbreaking toil for the odd backhander from farmers who were backwards in coming forwards with the backhanders, which they wouldn't backdate.

Winding the clock back myself, I can look back on my background and upbringing in a cottage with back-to-back outside services and no back door. Situated in a small backwater and backing onto a backcloth of backwoods it was my playground. At play, I had to learn the difference between back and front. No one used the front of a tree as a toilet, always the back.

As I grew older, I'd put my back into nothing, had no backbone, and expected others to stay off my back. When I played rugby, they made me play forward and not at back. While not playing at back, but at forward, I broke my collarbone.

Back out of work, I spotted an advertisement on the back page of a newspaper to back a winner and join the Met Police.

Policemen, it was expected, backed other policemen up. I never turned my back on this commitment: they all got back up. Behind senior officer's backs, I took a back seat, which got their backs up and I'd go back and forth between Indian and Chinese restaurants that backed onto back alleys until the backfire that ended it. The Indians and Chinese were glad that I didn't come back at all.

Then I went back to sea until my back went. Since then, I've not looked back. While the wind was backing, my seagoing pension fund was backing up with riches and I've got my own contributions back and a bit extra, too.

Backing this, I've got a good mate who has never turned his back on me, won't back down, or back out, and has never backed a horse, though he might have stuck his back teeth into the curried back quarters of a few animals while round the back, in back kitchens, back then, with me.

It's amazing what some folk keep in the back of their mind.

Always, Bob Back.

An Epistle From The Everlasting Love Potion Emporium

48 Permafrost Road
Corby under Snow
Nr Carlisle
HA 69 96 HA
Cumbria
Email: evlastlopoem@hotmail.com
Ordering Centre Telephone: 01228305603
Friday 24th March 2006.

Our ref: W.D.M.G./M.R.D.B.

Dear Sir,

In a world where so many gullible sufferers of erectile dysfunction fall to the lure of 'snake oil' panaceas, we find it rewarding each time a rejuvenation seeker asks for a supply of PINWINKLE, one of our pure, organic, proven products. Coming your way soon under plain-brown wrapper is the one-year's supply of PINWINKLE 'The Everlasting Love-potion Emporium's' super-strength, easily-swallowed capsules of horny goat weed that you desire.

Horny goat weed is our most sought after product. You need have no fears of its efficacy; it is 'top quality' and it will make you extremely sexually aroused and bountiful.

All users notice an immediate effect on swallowing their first dose. Thereafter, a permanent, ready-to-use erection occurs on the mere thought or transitory whim of sex: claims that the manufacturers of Viagra and Levitra would like to make.

Do not confuse our product with inferior horny goat root, which the Chinese refer to as Yin Yang, Wo-up-biff, loosely meaning 'plant

54

of licentious goats'. It is addictive, encourages parsimony and produces prolonged and painful erections. Unscrupulous backstreet vendors push this poor imitation. Beware!

Our horny goat weed, or Epimedium, is a pungent, ornamental herb found in Asia, and the Mediterranean. Legend has it that the herder, who first noticed how his goats became stimulated by the plant, ejaculated the words horny goat weed, in a moment of inspiration, much like that of the scientist who cracked the conundrum and spouted Eureka. This was the reputed exclamation of Archimedes when, after long study, he discovered a method of detecting the amount of alloy mixed with the gold in the crown of the king of Syracuse.

Such were the rampant antics of the males, and the submissive, tails-to-the-side ways of the females, not only did the rockets fire, they entered the stockade through the gun-ports, broached the doors of the armoury and blew up the barracks as well.

Indeed, no animal or man was safe from an unwanted sexual coupling on those olden, horny-goat-weed-strewn hillsides. Horses mated with cows and vice versa, producing jumarts; goats mated with sheep and vice versa, producing geeps and shoats, Biblical tales confirming the presence of such nightmarish beasts. Had it been a known pastime then, the area would surely have become the 'dogging' centre of the ancient world.

Not so dead scrolls from those climes claim that octogenarian men competed with teenage rivals for the favours of available maidens. Dodder and groan as they might, those priapic coffin-dodgers knew horny goat weed as the herb that, when taken at the optimum dosages, gave their backbones renewed, bow-like springiness, and erections which were magnificent, stiffer and longer lasting. There is little doubt that those old men had appeal; the scrolls go as far as to suggest the usual outcome of those contests: 'After rubbing massive amounts of Spanish fly into flaccid penises, youthful Adonises, now brandishing blood-gorged, swingeing phalli, were often cast aside in favour of their elders.'

Reputable supplement companies like us, sure of our product's efficacy and potency, have retained the provocative name.

Horny goat weed received the name Epimedium because it is similar to a plant found in the primeval, Asian kingdom of Media, now a part of Iran. Epimedium is a genus of many related plant species used for medicinal purposes, including Shagittatum, Epimedium brevicornum, Epimedium koreanum, and Grippie-get and Ban-inleak, which teuchter men swear by.

Horny goat weed also has a history as a traditional treatment for disorders of the kidneys, limb-joints and the liver. Specialists treating drinkers prone to using blasphemous rhetoric when 'it's their shout', use it is a psychological, hand-to-pocket extender, but its principle use is as an aphrodisiac and to combat fatigue and lethargy.

Having an interest in old Scottish words and sayings, you will already understand radgie gait weed.

William McGonnagle, a great and respected Scot, wrote of the herbal phenomena in his acclaimed ode, 'Ayont Deil's Parritch':

Bodsy Nickie Ben,
Een boggled an glowering,
Quat deil's parritch
For radgie gait weed.
Nou, he seeks the queanies
The bicks an the hallackets,
Wae his pintle streekit
He's taupie, the bawheid.

A Scottish study investigated the therapeutic effect of horny goat weed on 22 male, asexual porridge addicts, suffering from drink-purchasing-related blasphemous tendencies. Research showed that the weed had a sex-enhancing effect on them, reduced porridge dependency, increased generosity, palpably reduced the unseemly, offensive utterances, which had poured forth from the mouths of the stricken individuals, even when they were not sexually aroused, thus improving the quality of life of their often ear-shocked, despondent, drinking partners. This is proof that the herb's mechanism has more than one action.

Research has also shown that horny goat weed inhibits A.C.H.E (alchoholinesterarse), an enzyme that inactivates cholinergic neurotransmitters, linking blasphemy with sex.

For example: sexual arousal activates the brain's cholinergic neurotransmitters when engaged in the sexual-arousal process and switches off the multi-profano neurotransmitters responsible for blasphemous tendencies; therefore, the two should never appear simultaneously. Thus, the pathological need to burst out with streams of expletives during the sex act ceases, the subject becoming both aroused and free to choose vocabulary that is more suitable to the occasion.

As a boosting supplement to increase your sexual desire, ability, endurance, performance, to reduce blasphemous outbursts in pubs and clubs and to direct your hand to a pocket, we recommend 22 capsules of PINWINKLE taken on rising each morning, thus ensuring total control whilst awake. For more immediate action before sex, we recommend an extra dose of 40 capsules 30 minutes before your activities.

Our aim is to steady your hand, get it into your pockets without any blaspheming, and get your sexual-machinery up and running again. The estimate of your yearly requirement and the average sexual activity envisaged for someone of your age, fitness and pathological parsimony: sex thrice nightly, twice weekly and pocket-finding ease over the course of 52 weeks: $3 \times 2 \times 52 \times 40 = 12480$ of our super-strength-formula capsules.

Our prices are competitive, when compared to Viagra and Levitra, and contain memory enhancers. At £1per hundred, you can obtain an annual supply for the competitive price of £124.80. Confirm your order, claim an additional 10% reduction and arrange C.O.D on orders over £125 with one quick call to our ordering centre. Tell a friend.

Yours truly,

Dick Wilting

Managing Director, Marketing

Tales Of My Littles Of Ruthwell Village, Dumfriesshire, Scotland,

and some other villagers

From a book written by Helen McFarlan, wife of the Ruthwell Church minister from 1871-1889, I have taken the following quote. Forty years ago one might meet old men and women walking the Ruthwell soil, grim in aspect, serious-minded, resenting the very idea of a joke, scorning 'the joy of living' as a sin, and all of them imbued with the fixed idea that they and their forbears were incomparably the best type on the face of the earth.

I do not think there were many moments in my life when I was ever that seriously minded enough to resent or resist a joke; indeed, I make up a few myself. I enjoyed living my life to the full, but never thought that I was one of the best types on the face of the earth. Others will have to confirm whether I am grim of aspect. My sins I will pay for at another time, and at another place!

What I am saying: there were grey, unsmiling villagers present during my upbringing in the village, but I was unaffected by them.

My family tree, traceable back to 1710 with Latter Day Saints, tells me in that year John Little was born at Burnfoot, Rigshaw, Moffat. He had two sons, Matthew and John. My Littles are descendents of Matthew. I am interested to know of Rigshaw. According to my Scottish dictionary, a rig is a thin piece of land; a shaw is a natural wood. The word Rigshaw explains what the location once looked like. I have never found reference to the place on any map I've seen.

Lochmaben came next on the family's progression towards Ruthwell, the first James Little born there, in 1768. He married Jean Gunion, fathered six children, his first son, James, was born in 1799.

In 1841, we find James (1799), his wife, (Janet Boyd) and four children at the Thwaite farm, Ruthwell, where he was probably a farmhand. In 1851 they lived at Churchgate cottages, one-hundred yards from the church. Two other children were born there: William, my great grandfather, and Elizabeth. Janet died in 1884. I have a photograph of her as an elderly woman with four grandchildren by her side. There is no certain knowledge of why the family moved to Churchgate, just a hint that James did some work for the then minister, Henry Duncan.

William was a talented quoiter. He lived only 48 years, dying of TB in 1892. In the 1920s, my father saw the cabinet of cups and trophies he had won, in the cottage at Churchgate. I would like to have known him. My two grandsons had a living great-grandfather, my father, William, 95, until 2010, yet they seldom thought to pay him a visit.

My grandfather, Ebenezer, must have inherited some of his father's talent for hurling objects accurately. His skill was throwing stones at and hitting moving or stationary objects: scurrying rabbits and hares and roosting birds. Family lore is clearer on this topic: my father repeating the tales, as if he hadn't told them before, when he had, hundreds of times!

Ebenezer's skill is worth repeating here. He could hit a running rabbit or hare with a round stone, his favourite, and bring the beasts down, with unerring accuracy. He would also knock crows, when they were young and juicy, from the branches of trees in the 'Crow wood', with stones. The kill he would tie together by the legs and send by bus to a Birmingham game-dealer, to become the main ingredient in that much-loved Black Country delicacy, crow pie.

My grandfather worked as a trainee cobbler, in Mundell's village shop, then as a horseman at the Castle Milk Estate, owned by the prosperous Buchanan Jardine Family. His skill with horses took him to Gloucester, where he drove a six-in-hand hearse. He married and settled in Cardiff. I was born there, as was my father and dear Aunt May. A brother and sister followed Ebenezer south, both marrying and settling in Cardiff, raising children, strengthening the gene pool of the principality, a Little.

In 1940, as the bombing of Cardiff began, Grampy, as I knew him, Granny and May moved back to the village. My mother and I followed soon after. My father enlisted in the army. He was missing from our lives for much of the next four years.

My Ruthwell life began in 1941. I have few memories of my babyhood in Ruthwell. Perhaps the first of these was my mother carrying me, in my grandfather's cottage, and me stretching my small, unknowing hand towards and touching the lit bulb, it burning my tender fingertips. I remember the COSSOR, an old valve wireless, and the sombre, wartime announcements listened to by my elders. I remember the war ending and the rejoicing. I remember, days later, catching the bus to school at the Glebe and my father getting off, kit bag over his shoulder, demobbed, his army days over.

In a cottage further down the village lived the Dalrymple family, relations through a sister of my grandfather. Brothers Will and Tom were rabbit and mole catchers. I remember seeing the regular catches: dozens of rabbits, snared in the Broom explosives factory, managed by Imperial Chemical Industries, where I also served a part of my apprenticeship as an electrician. Will and Tom gutted them in the garden, a gory spectacle, the innards thrown into a hole. Nearly all cottages had outside toilets, the bucket contents regularly buried alongside the rabbit guts. The soil must have been most fertile. I recall rhubarb was a prolific and tall cropper.

Will and Tom killed moles rather more carefully, using arsenic pellets, speared onto pins, before inserting the poison into worms, for placing in the underground run of the animal.

The only place the village had that young men could congregate of an evening was the cobbler's shop, then in the hands of William Herbert. Heb, as he was known, made and resoled clogs, repaired shoes and boots, sold lemonade, cigarettes tobacco and newspapers. Heb had a wonderful ability to start arguments, the ensuing debates easily heard halfway up the village, as was the clatter of dominoes on his counter.

Apart from death, there were other guarantees in Ruthwell life. One was that churchgoers would leave their cottages at ten thirty of a Sunday morning and walk the glebe loaning to attend the eleven o'clock service. Another was that non-churchgoers would rush from their cottages to catch the twenty-past six bus to Dumfries on a

Saturday night. The churchgoer would return home silent, fulfilled, the Saturday night revellers, filled with booze, noisy and drunk.

Tramping flounders (flooks) was an annual, August event. Then, the fish were at their fattest. The river Lochar was the venue, at the Brow Well, where Rabbie Burns went for a cure but didn't find it. Walking line abreast, bare of foot, trampers paddled along against the muddy flow until they felt the slippery flooks back beneath a foot; sometimes, trampers caught two, one under each, then there was a struggle to remain upright, especially the women, howling with false fright.

The catch wriggling but safely trapped, the tramper would then dip a hand into the water to tightly take hold of the flook by the head, remove it from the water, and guide a metal wire through the gills for secure carrying.

Some Ruthwell Littles had gifts, but never valuable possessions. But their diets were healthy: rabbits, snared, long-netted or ferreted, then curried, roasted or stewed. Flook fillets, in season, rolled in oatmeal. Shore mushrooms, the tastiest of any. All consumed with yummy, well-fertilised, garden-grown vegetables, from plots adjacent to the healthy rhubarb crop!

Nautical Section

Table of Contents

Life After Death

For a moment, my spirit felt uplifted that spring morning. I thought the mists dulling my mind in the wake of my wife's death and funeral were clearing. The sun was shining brightly through the kitchen window, hitting my face. I felt its warmth was reviving me.

It was a wonderful feeling, but the joy I felt was short lived. Moving to stand closer to the kitchen sink, with one hand gripping it, I saw through the window the wilderness that was once the flower garden, glorious when in bloom. The angle of the sun's rays threw long shadows to highlight the jungle of thistles and weeds flourishing there. In my other hand was a large gin and tonic; the hand was shaking uncontrollably and the drink was spilling.

Initially, I found it strange that I was drinking gin: its smell had always made me retch. Then the waves of agony hit me again and I reeled, as I guess I had on many mornings following the death of Ruth. Since then I had been wallowing in self-pity, I was sure, and wishing that I had been taken and not my beloved Ruth.

I stared towards the drink for some time, attempting to ascertain why it should be there at all. When my shoulders began to shake uncontrollably, I poured it into the sink. Watching it trickle away down the plughole, I thought this is where my life is going, too.

Turning, I entered the hallway and looked at my reflection in the long mirror. Mirrors do not lie; I was a mess. Pricklier looking than the unkempt flower garden, I had many days growth of facial hair, which covered razor nicks and cuts varying in age, length and depth. I had been bald for years, now there were scrapes and bruises visible on my pate, where it must have collided with hard objects. Grey tufts of hair were growing down my neck and spilling over a grubby shirt collar. My eyes were bleary, dark-ringed, watery and unquestionably sad. The clothes I wore were stained and crumpled. I had obviously been sleeping in them: my body odour stank. It was quickly evident that I was flirting with alcoholism: I had seen it all before and had sniffed the stench emanating from the sweat of other gin-swilling unfortunates.

If I were already an alcoholic, it struck me that the condition that I had found myself in would be more painful to rectify than the removal of the supermarket bags filled to overflowing with empty bottles that had collected in the garage. I looked at the calendar with disbelief; six months had passed since the funeral. I began to weep.

I didn't reach for the bottle. There could be no return for the disorientating mists. I made my mind up there and then that there wouldn't be.

That afternoon the shakes began to rack my body and my mouth remained permanently dry. My body was crying out for a fix, but it wasn't going to get one.

I had found, during my career on deck in the Merchant Navy, (from deck cadet through to Captain), that 'Old Mother Gin' had an appealing bosom, which attracted and took over the lives of many poor sots with whom I had sailed. They were from different backgrounds, in every department and they paid a mind-paining price, damaged their careers, lives and their livers.

I could have gone down that route and looked into the depths of too many empty spirit bottles, before depositing them unceremoniously through a porthole into the sea. I was teetotal, had been since my days as a cadet. Whilst a cadet, drinking too much alcohol had encouraged an event over which I couldn't control. I vowed then I would never let it happen again.

There were times during long voyages, when it would have been so easy to give in to loneliness and seek comfort in the arms of the 'Old Mother' or some other spirit that I found more palatable. But I had seen the horrifying consequences of shipmates affected by 'Delirium Tremens'. 'The 'Dreaded Lergy', the seafarer's version, was never kinder.

I expected, therefore, to be visited by mind-ravaging hallucinations; elephants of the pinker variety, snakes, fangs darting, their sinister, swirling coils winding around my lower limbs, other mind disturbing apparitions sitting at the foot of my bed, and they did call. My pitiful, anguished cries travelled beyond the confines of my bedroom, but being without close neighbours to my cottage near Gorebridge, south of Edinburgh, they went unheard and I suffered alone.

Three days later, only a minor shake remained, but an untroubled and full night's sleep was still far off. Then it suddenly struck me that I, Humphrey MacDonald, was alone in the world, without son or daughter, devoid of anyone closely related to me. Without Ruth, there was absolutely no one at all I could turn to.

We had tried for a family early in our marriage. Nothing happened. Then her work in the Scottish Office seemed more important to her. There was a time when I thought that Ruth knew she couldn't conceive children, but hadn't said. To make sure I was okay, in case she ever changed her mind, I went, in some foreign port or other, to a clinic and had my sperm count tested. It was a positive result.

Three days after resigning 'the pledge', and compos mentos enough to switch the television on, I was watching 'Scotland Today'. The programme was showing how Glasgow's Govan had risen from the abyss of poverty, drunken-violence and squalor-stricken streets to a sought after area in which to live. I recalled being aboard a ship drydocking in a yard there as a first trip cadet and the short relationship...the one-night stand I had with a Jessie Wilson. I was but a boy. Guilt troubled me the next day. After all, I was the son of a Presbyterian minister and fearful of sinning.

Being the deck cadet, the youngest person amongst the officer ranks, it had fallen on me to telephone the Southern General Hospital nurses' home to enquire if any nurses fancied coming down to the ship for a party. Of course, some did, free drink, music and dancing the attraction. Jessie was amongst them.

Jessie was a couple of years older than I was, very attractive, small of stature and slightly overweight. I never thought I had a chance with her. I had heard one or two of the officers saying they fancied wheeling her off to their cabins. I also heard them telling some nurses that I was a cherry boy. That soubriquet, they thought, would reduce my chances of scoring with a nurse, leaving an extra choice open for them to do so.

It didn't work. I suppose I was a bit of a trophy in a way. Jessie won and dragged me to my cabin where she seduced me. I wasn't used to alcohol and was a little tipsy, for sure, and so was Jessie. My cherry was there for the picking and sure enough, it went. I remember being at the brunt of officers' humour for most of the next voyage. For months afterwards, I considered writing to Jessie, but in the end, I didn't for fear of the additional scorn I would endure from officers who thought windups entertaining. My parents wouldn't have taken fondly to Jessie either. Of that, I was sure.

Then I had the crazy thought. Was it possible that there might have been a child, the product of our lovemaking that night? It was fanciful I knew and doubts surfaced thick and fast. Jessie had been a nurse, after all; she would have been taking the pill. If she wasn't, then as a nurse, she ought to have known the next best way of not having a child. It couldn't be…but then.

An old Merchant Navy discharge book pinpointed exactly the date of the drydocking in Govan and my initiation to sex. Suddenly, my mind was racing and armed with this knowledge, I went directly to the records office at the top of Leith Walk in Edinburgh. In the births section there, I found an entry that almost blew my mind. A Jessica Wilson had registered the birth of a Donald Humphrey Wilson almost nine months to the day later and at the same address that I remembered all these years later where Jessie lived.

I packed a small case and took the train through to Glasgow. I had already planned where I would stay and took a taxi to the Airport Hotel near Renfrew, which was not a stone's throw from where I remembered Jessie's address was.

I could see the improvements, the updating and refurbishment of tenement blocks, since my last visit thirty years previously. Now they looked more like yuppie homes.

I decided to hang around for a while and walk up and down the streets, look around, see if I could spot a small, greying lady who looked a bit like the remnants of a memory that was continually invading my thinking. Somehow, I feared knocking on the door of that address.

On one of my walks, I saw an insalubrious looking taxi office with metal grills protecting the windows. 'Big D Taxis', proprietor: Donald Humphrey Wilson it said on the sign. The discovery stopped me in my tracks.

Through the door, I could hear a male voice speaking into what I thought must be a microphone, relaying to taxi drivers waiting for trade the message where to go to pick up a customer, and the metallic rogers of the responses. It could be a worker, I thought, and not what I had hoped.

The pushing open of that scruffy door and entering the confines of a taxi office was what I had to do. I could not leave the area without knowing.

The door ajar, I saw the stockily built male person sitting behind a desk littered with plastic coffee cups, carry out wrappers, a writing pad and a beaker of pens. The man was holding a microphone up to his face, but he turned his head towards me. I was looking into the same eyes that I had seen looking back at me from the mirror on many a morning.

Donald must have seen the same, for he said to me, in a slow voice filled with emotion, 'Dad, I wondered if you would ever call. Mum told me exactly what you looked like. Come on in.'

Behind Donald, I saw a woman sitting at a desk, writing into a ledger. She had her back to me, but I noticed quickly she was gray-headed and small of stature. This was a family business.

The Loss Of The Nellie Dene

The Nellie Dene fished; her stern was to the Atlantic Ocean, darkening and ominous. Clouds raced over the horizon towards her, increasing black and heavy in the grip of the deepening low-pressure area. Night was falling and the scavenging seabirds accompanying her began winging towards the shore.

Her skipper, looking towards the threatening storm, his forehead creased in a worried frown, said to his helmsman, 'We'll have to lift the nets and make a run for it.' Tossing a thumb over his shoulder in the direction of the threat, he said. 'That there looks nasty, and it wasn't mentioned on this morning's forecast.'

The skipper stopped the Nelly's engine and ordered the nets hoisted aboard. Within minutes of emptying the haul onto the deck, she began to lift uneasily in the swell. Soon she was running at full-speed before the freshening westerly, only a solitary storm petrel for company. Her old timbers creaked mournfully; her engine raced as the screw cleared water, and her crew, sorting the catch with their life jackets handy, watched the weather quickly worsen and listened to Nellie's groans with trepidation.

None of the hands, or the Nellie Dene, built as an inshore fishing vessel, had experienced the ferocity of an Atlantic storm. She, like them, had always fished within sight of land and an easy run from the safety of her homeport. EEC fishing policies dictated that they take her elsewhere to fish for within-quota fish.

The skipper tapped the barometer and watched its plunge. 'It's going down fast. That's a severe storm and we're a two hours run from the Minches and the lea of the land. I wish those chaps at the met office could get it right a bit more often.' The helmsman, wrestling with the lurching wheel, heard him, but was too busy to reply.

The wind-speed indicator whirled crazily. If it registered gale-force eleven, Nellie was in danger of floundering. The wind was already whooping and howling around the bridge, whipping wave tops to spume, lashing spray onto decks, and blowing a threnody through her scant rigging. She was lifting more and then letting herself down into the ever-heightening, oily-green troughs.

The wind reached Gale-force-eleven as darkness engulfed completely. Waves began tumbling over her, lifting her up, then crashing her down, dashing the haul, ready in stacked boxes for the morning market, over the side and into the threatening sea.

The skipper didn't wait for a brief moment of calm. He crossed the lurching bridge holding onto what he could, reached the ship-to-shore radio, picked up the handset, and cried: 'Mayday, mayday.' He hadn't experienced gale-force eleven before, but he'd seen enough. Nellie and her crew were in danger. For his trouble, the ship-to-shore gave him an earful of static and squelch, He was unsure anyone had heard the distress message.

The storm raged and Nellie made little headway, her screw hardly in the water. Then the bilge pump packed up and she began to take-in water in the engine room through sprung timbers. The engine grumbled, then suddenly stopped. Nellie began to ride lower in the water. Without way, waves battered into her relentlessly, tossing her like a cork.

The helmsman lashed the wheel midships. Without way, there was no steering. The skipper and his helmsman stood holding onto the door of the swinging wheelhouse, peering into the darkness looking for a friendly light: the sound of the air-sea rescue helicopter above the roar of the wind. The Nellie Dene's navigation lights flickered. 'I'd better get another Mayday off before the batteries die,' the skipper said, turning.

'Don't forget our last dead-reckoning position,' the helmsman told him before letting out the weak laugh of a man facing danger.

The lights went out. The skipper and helmsman left the bridge. Feeling their way aft in the dark, they clung onto a superstructure rail. Nellie heaved frantically. Low in the water now, waves broke over her, tugged at them, threatening to wash them away, salt spray burning their eyes. The inflatable life raft lay in its cradle set on the afterdeck; it was their only hope. The other two crewmembers gathered around it, wearing their oilskins and their life jackets.

The highest wave of the storm crested. Atop was Nelly, her white superstructure stark against a troubled sky. The huge, watery hand of the wave held her there for one brief moment, like a chalice offered to King Neptune. Instead of riding down the leading edge of the wave with hope, she tottered and spilled backwards tumbling down it with none. The following wave smashed over her, bashed the cover from the hold, filling it. Her bow tipped forward, she prepared for the lunge to the bottom.

The wash on the afterdeck lifted the inflatable capsule from its cradle, and floated it over the gunnels. The skipper grunted as he pulled sharply on the rope attached to the release mechanism on the capsule. It opened like a clamshell, and allowed the compressed air to hiss its promise of survival into the inflatable. It inflated in seconds, its shape becoming apparent quickly before their eyes. The skipper leapt first as Nellie went 'down by the head' and the stern began to soar. He landed squarely on the tent-like structure flapping above the inflatable. He felt the weight of other bodies hit his back. He counted three.

Gripping to anything and everything, hanging on, cold, the skipper and his three crewmembers felt no safer. Nellie's stern towered above them, the swell taking them close in, crashing them into her keel, crusty with marine growth, then out again. Then, they watched her quietly, without protest, slide slowly beneath the waves.

The next wave fell about them, tearing them from the inflatable before they had located the entrance to the survival tent. In the dark, their faces and hands stood out stark in the blackness, illuminated bleakly by the pitiful saltwater-operated lamps on the life jackets. Bobbing around, spinning, going under, gulping seawater mixed with diesel fuel, spluttering, shouting, they looked for a sight of another. Ropes hanging from the inflatable trailed in the water. The skipper caught hold of one and shouted, 'Here.'

Bulky life jackets supporting white faces moved slowly towards the voice, hands and arms digging into the rearing water for propulsion. The high sea kept washing them apart, but each grasped a trailing lifeline and began dragging themselves closer to the inflatable, now rearing and careering in a sea wanting to take them beneath it like Nellie. The skipper was finally able to pull the inflatable around until the survival tent's entrance was opposite him.

Folded inside was a rope ladder. He hauled it out, allowing the end to drop into the water. It wouldn't make entering the inflatable much easier. Hauling himself up with all his remaining strength, he scrambled up and over the edge of the inflatable, tumbling into the interior. The most frightened was the youngest fisherman who shivered and moaned. The skipper settled him with rough words and hauled him in.

His helmsman went up and over next. Peering out into the storm lashed darkness they looked for the other. There was no light, no blotch of a white face, and no flailing white hands stood out on the darkness of the sea.

The contents of pouches on every inflatable include survival gear. 'Search for the torch and the flares,' ordered the skipper trying to beat life into his hands. Numb fingers, blown on and swore at, tore open the pouches on the sides of the inflatable. With an illumination flare in hand, the skipper opened the tent entrance, and pulled on the igniter cord. The flare began to crackle, then, assume its full brilliance.

Towards the edge of the flares range, fifty feet distant, a life jacket bobbed in the sea, its occupant's head hanging lifeless. 'Hold this,' the skipper ordered the young lad, 'like this, high.' Out of the other tent door, the skipper and the helmsman leaned over the edge of the inflatable and paddled with their hands. Slowly, they made progress towards their life-belted shipmate. At times, he drifted over the crest of a wave and was lost to view. Other times, he was close enough for grabbing, only for the sea to toss him in another direction.

Slowly, inexorably, the paddling hands won the race, grabbed his life jacket and pulled him aboard. His face was ashen, but he still breathed. A deep gash creased his forehead and blood trickled down his face. The sea had thrown him against Nellie before she slipped away.

The skipper fired a distress flare in wild hope. It hung in the sky on a parachute, but no one believed in imminent rescue. At first light, things might be different, if someone had received the Mayday message.

The injured man regained consciousness and retched salt water. He was sodden and chilled, but no different to the others. Among the survival packages were easily opened cans of food that warmed chemically. All feasted on the contents, gulping them down with a ravenous relish, hands clasping the tins, the only source of heat. All shivered uncontrollably in the huddle together, absorbing the artificial warmth from the tins.

The storm had abated somewhat by first light. It was then that the steady drone and whapping... the sound signature of the sea-king helicopter's turbo-jet engine and blades... brought the skipper's head through the tent flap. The helicopter was turning towards them and descending. Soon the downdraft from the blades stung their eager, gawping faces, and the rescue man on the end of the wire rope lowered towards them.

Like all saviours, they were welcome visitors.

Captain Stone's Folly

Captain Peter Inigo Stone had not been compos mentos on many days during the voyage; as Master of the cargo vessel Mistral, he had lengthy periods of staggering drunkenness and was never aware of his fellow officer's level of disrespect for him. Behind his back, the deck and engineer officers called him 'The Pist One'. Using his initials and surname, they had concocted the sobriquet, which highlighted his hard-drinking reputation.

Captain Stone had served his apprenticeship as a deck cadet with the 'Brass Bell Line', then serving them for another forty years as deck officer and Master. After an initial burst of enthusiasm, which saw him achieve glorious promotion to Master of the company's only passenger ship, boredom had set in. It seemed from the moment he began to command general cargo vessels he had tumbled downhill into the comforting but exhausting arms of 'Old Mother Gin'.

He had looked into the depths of many empty gin bottles, before lofting them from a porthole into the sea. His alcohol consumption had often brought on Delirium Tremens. Mind-ravaging convulsions and appearances of disturbing hallucinations--- elephants in traditional pink and other horrifying images sitting at the foot of his bunk, while he lay, unable to sleep. He had suffered alone. All crew heard, without compassion, the pitiful, anguished cries coming from his cabin.

Homeward bound with a cargo of Indian jute, Mistral steamed northwards into a stormy Bay of Biscay. A deepening low-pressure weather system to the north of Cape Finnistere was creating driving, force-ten winds. The dark, menacing sea was rising steadily, the air becoming spume laden, to fall like rain on the deck. The Mistral had ridden such conditions many times during her long service with the company. Now she ploughed through the waves gallantly, but at a reduced five knots.

The Minstral was an ancient rusting vessel whose plates of welded Scottish steel had worn perilously thin during a lifetime in which she had traversed a million miles of ocean. Built around 1965, in Harland and Wolf's yard in Belfast, she was overdue becoming an impermanent fixture in a marine knackery. She was a heavy-fuel-burning diesel-engined trampship. She had hard-working engineers, who perpetually complained about the amount of work involved keeping her going. Nowadays, a rarely achieved maximum speed of eleven knots required a wind off her stern and a following sea. That optimistic promise of speed usually caused trepidation amongst the crew, especially the engineers who had to sort out and refit any pieces falling off the main engine, instead of excitement.

The increasing swell was causing Mistral to heave and buck violently. All crew found the conditions uncomfortable. It had shaken Captain Stone out of his alcoholic stupor, alerting him to the due docking of Mistral, in Hull, in seven days time, weather permitting, and that he had to get back quickly onto the wagon and appear in command: the marine superintendent would pay him a visit to collect the ship's logbook and his voyage report. Captain Stone knew it was paramount he gave the impression of total control over his ship and he began preparations.

He had his own well-tested way to rid himself of his alcoholic need: reducing his intake over five days to none and spending time walking the bridge wings, the bracing wind tugging his ruddy face to a healthier glow and drinking copious mugs of sweet, black coffee.

His white uniforms stank with the rotten smell of gin, secreted in unhealthy sweat through laboured pores. His Asian steward would launder and press all his clothes and clean his cabin, removing all traces of alcohol, except what was normal in his cabinet to offer visitors from shoreside. The cabin would appear neat and tidy, like any other teetotal Captains' on entering port. His spare blue uniform he had kept clean and reassuringly fragrant, donning it only when greeting the Humber pilot and to appear smart in port.

Some neglected Paperwork he had to give his attention. After a couple of days 'off the booze', he waded into the waiting pile. It was routine until he came upon the agents receipt for oil and water bunkered in Aden. He could not understand why his First Mate hadn't filled Number1 water tank. Company instructions were to top up all water tanks in provider ports.

His opinion of his First Mate, Dai Morgan, a Welshman, wasn't brilliant. He thought him a prickly, ginger headed and dishonest Celt, whose pair of high, outstanding cheekbones, hook nose, close-set eye-sockets from which a pair of dark, devious eyes peered, gave him a gypsy-like distrustful appearance. He had often recited to himself these thoughts in the childish rhyme 'Taffy was a Welshman, Taffy was a thief', truly believing it.

He knew his old Scots Chief Engineer, Roddy MacDonald, would have fuel in reserve, having fiddled his oil consumption figures. An extra few tons of bunkers up his sleeve would show his engine always worked to the optimum expected of it. He had never asked Roddy if he received baksheesh from suppliers for bunkering less tonnage than what the company paid. He just guessed he did.

Captain Stone's last loading instructions had taken him to the hot, stifling, fly infested port of Madras where, as instructed, he loaded a bulky and fibrous cargo of jute. Here the company's turbaned agent, with a name he often had difficulty pronouncing, was Sanbumba Sanu Singh. He had always considered him to be a 'dodgy chappy' and well capable of offering bribes to the errant Morgan to stow aboard something that wasn't legal. The Singh chappy had even offered him, Commodore of the Fleet Captain Stone, a night out in a house of ill repute, which he had declined. He knew the situations in which lesser seagoing mortals found themselves and the risks they took when they had a run ashore. After all, he had done the same things himself, when he was young and in the days before he became a Captain.

The stench of the river and dock area, the shabby, rat infested, refuse-strewn streets of the crinkly tin and cardboard constructed shantytowns that surrounded the city and the sight of crippled children and blind beggars kept him ship bound. Strangely, he recalled, each time he'd docked in Madras, with Morgan as Mate, some of the sun-warped, paint-cracked crinkly tin roofs of the shantytowns suddenly adopted the colours of the shipping line, as new painting became evident. Recalling this made him surer that Morgan was up to something; if he had taken no water in that tank in Aden, then he was using it for some other reason....like smuggling.

The time spent in Madras was arduous for all. Warehouses ran out of stocks and the non-arrival of trains from the Jute growing regions over the creaky, internal rail systems and the unbearable heat caused unrest. He had taken solace in his cabin, which was more gracious than what other officers had; he had fans that moved the air about, giving the impression of coolness. Others had wind-scoops, fashioned from discarded five-gallon oil drums cut in two lengthwise, jutting from their portholes, hoping to promote the flow of air into their living quarters. They weren't as useless on passage with the ship's motion through the water causing a weak natural draught as they were in port.

He had spent his afternoons comfortably reclined in his hammock, on an open deck, beneath a protective fly net, with several large gin and tonics, an ice bucket and books about the sleuth Father Brown, that the padre from the local seaman's mission had brought him, his only company. He thought some of the villains the Father trailed and caught had distorted souls, as he thought Morgan had. On too many occasions, he'd slept there, under the influence, dreaming of crimes unimaginable and that he, as a sleuth, might trail criminals and apprehend perpetrators. Occasionally, dreaming of his dear wife and family interrupted his sleuthing fantasies; he had not had any leave for more than a year.

Although ultimately responsible, he'd taken no interest in the loading of his ship. The company paid others to do that. They would have sweated and complained. He was sure Morgan had sold ship's paint and was guilty of stashing some illegal drugs in the water tank. He was sure he had read something similar occurring in a Father Brown book, and how the Father had unravelled the complicated evidence to solve the crime.

Eight days after entering The Bay of Biscay, Mistral anchored in the Humber estuary.

Captain Stone expected to see the pilot cutter approach to drop off a pilot, as the tide turned. Standing on his bridge wing, the anchoring procedure completed, he was trying to look interested and important with small binoculars tight to his eyes. He was peering concernedly towards Mistral's Plimsoll line. He found it difficult to position his bulk over the bridge-wing railings to obtain a better view of the ship's marks; feeling giddy still, he dare not lean his bulky frame further out.

However, he had seen enough; he reckoned he didn't need to do any sleuthing, his experience at sea as a deck officer and twenty years as a master mariner was enough for him to know that something was amiss with the ship's loading: he was sure none of the Plimsoll line was visible above water.

The Minstral had loaded in the warm, buoyant seawater of the Indian Ocean and now lay at anchor in fresh. Even so, he mused, as he considered his findings: even a 'landlubber' on a dark night, with an additional smoke screen obscuring the evidence, might guess she was illegally below her marks. Had Morgan taken baksheesh from the dodgy Singh chappy in Madras to overload the ship, as well as using a water tank to smuggle? Evidence enough, he thought, to establish that Morgan was definitely dodgy and a criminal.

Lying at anchor now, Mistral waited to enter her discharge port of Hull and rode out the ebb tide, now swirling and eddying down a narrow, buoyed channel of the sprawling estuary. Her vertical bow required urgent treatment with a marine paint, as did her counter stern. A red-duster hung limply there, neglected on its jack-staff, filthy with the layered smoke of the long voyage.

The tawny-coloured, mud-infused current pushed her back and occasionally sideways against her rusty starboard anchor chain, causing resonant clangs, and her navigation lights winked as she danced to an easy tune. Puffs of black smoke occasionally drifted slowly skywards from her pencil thin funnel. This was the only indication from a distance of life aboard, as an Ag Wallah, an Asian engineroom fireman, flashed the auxiliary boiler to keep up steam. The black, soot-filled pall of smoke, without the presence of a breeze, descended to obscure briefly the upper superstructure. It was an idyllic midsummer evening, the sun having escaped over the horizon of a cloudless sky, leaving an afterglow without a full-blown, cloud-reflected sunset.

Almost upon the stroke of midnight, as predicted, the tide turned. A thin, crescent moon offering some pale light accompanied it and the spectre of a breeze, from no fixed direction, pushed gently through the winch wires. The turn of the tide was the signal for the pilot cutter to come alongside the ship. A sturdy, well-practised pilot deftly grabbed the Jacob's ladder and stepped neatly off the bobbing boat. The ship's Deck Sarang greeted him as he breasted the bulwarks after his lurching climb with a welcome helping hand and took him to the bridge.

From the bow, the anchor chain made clanking sounds as it wound itself around the windlass. The blast of air kicking over the engine in preparation for movements sounded from the engineroom vents. These were positive indications that the ship was being prepared to proceed up river and enter port.

Captain Stone greeted the Pilot with a firm shake of the hand as he entered the bridge door. 'Your well down below your marks captain' reported the Pilot instantly. 'With the draft you're drawing, I don't think I can risk getting you through the lock gates into the dock on this tide.'

All of a sudden, those gin and tonic hazy lazy days took on a different significance: responsibility for the delay rested with him. He immediately aborted the sailing.

The news of the two-day delay in docking, until the tide had risen by the expected eighteen inches, sped around the ship as the pilot departed the way he came. This information caused various amounts of concern among the officers. Usually, most officers would choose to be relieved on docking day, to head home for a well-earned spell of leave. Others may opt to stand by the ship whilst it discharged and loaded on the coast and then take their leave. The remainder of the crew, made up of Lascars, engaged in Chittagong some months previously, would stay with the ship.

The ship's mail arrived with the pilot cutter, sent on by the considerate company agent in Hull. It contained letters not only from loved ones. Company mail addressed to Captain Stone contained official, though unexpected, confirmation of his retirement on a company pension, the scrapping of the Minstral and the promotion of Morgan to the rank of Captain, for the forthcoming scrapping voyage back to India.

The Minstral would end her days in a bay just to the north of Mumbai. On a beach, with a gentle incline from the sea, winches would heave her, bit by bit, with stout hawsers, onto the shore, portions of her cut off with acetylene torches as she rose from the water, until reduced to piles of scrap metal.

Captain Stone sat quietly, taking in the changes soon to take over his life, reflecting upon any joys he may have had as master of the Mistral and his life at sea. He thought of the balmy, shimmering at times Pacific Ocean and the dolphins that would appear and criss-cross the boughs of ships he had known well. He considered the quiet, the solitude of clear moonlit, star enshrouded nights when he thought he was looking back to the beginning of time.

He thought of the friends he'd made on the Pacific Islands and the evenings he'd spent listening to the islanders singing. He particularly remembered, in Nuku'alofa, the capital of Tonga, the islanders singing in their tribal language. That event had brought tears to his old, yellowing eyes. These were the sights he would no longer see and the sounds he would no longer hear. Then he heard the whoops of joy coming from Morgan's cabin positioned directly beneath his and it annoyed him that one he was trying to prove a crook should take his position.

Captain Stone thought for a time and planned a course of action to gather more evidence that Morgan was carrying contraband of one form or another in a water tank, which he would have to remove as Number 1 hold completely emptied of jute products. For surely he would not want to take it back to India?

He wondered what Morgan's leave arrangements were. The company had requested that he could either remain aboard until the final sailing or take a few days leave. He thought Morgan must soon decide between staying onboard to oversee the removal of whatever he had concealed in the tank and taking some leave.

Congratulating Morgan on his promotion wouldn't come easy, he thinking him unworthy of it, but he needed that information to help prove his suspicions.

The compliment of officers aboard amounted to nine in total and they all seemed to have congregated in Morgan's cabin. A case of already-cooled canned beer was open on his desk. Captain Stone detected a cabin-party atmosphere as he stood outside the curtained doorway. He heard a voice say, 'Aren't you going to invite The Pistone down for a drink?' Not thinking it had anything to do with him, he knocked out of courtesy before forcing his bulk through the curtain.

He smiled at the assembled throng but refused the beer Morgan offered him.

There was some of the convivial banter usual on ships. When in the mood, he would usually join in. He gave them news of his retirement and suffered the puns of those who suggested lewd uses for the hours he would have to fill, in his role as a husband, and not as a retired master mariner.

He slipped in his congratulations to Morgan with the additional aside. 'Mr Morgan will be first off the boat now that he's promoted. He'll need to buy four gold bands for his uniform cuffs, whilst he's on leave in Cardiff.' It received the snarled response for which he had designed the aside.

'I'm a single man, Captain. I've no need to take leave. I'll be gladly working by as Mate until I take over as Captain for the scrapping voyage. I know a decent marine tailor in Hull. I'll buy a new uniform to go with my new command.'

In almost every case of a ship entering a British port, the first person to board is a customs officer. They have several duties that include sealing the ship's bonded store, thus preventing the removal of duty-free goods, tobacco and alcohol whilst in port. They would then interview all personnel declaring duty free purchases and imported goods on the manifest and claim any duty due.

Clearing customs was usually a painless process, with seasoned customs officers encouraging personnel into lower valuations of their declared goods so they did not attract duty. However, on occasions, a notorious 'black gang' would board. These were trainee custom officers dressed in go-anywhere black overalls, who traditionally tore a ship apart in their quest to find hidden duty-free goods, which in most cases were tobacco products and alcohol. Sometimes they were successful, departing happily with a carton or two of cigarettes as prizes. They looked in all the traditional places of easy access for them as well as a culprit. Rarely if ever did they take the lid from a storage tank, unless they had a tip off.

It was also commonplace that they would pay particular attention to Asian crewed ships. Poor pay has those crews subsidising their wages with a little contraband smuggling, usually in the form of cigarettes, which they would sell to dockers for a considerable profit. Asian crew usually purchased goods for resale at a profit in India: old-fashioned wooden roller mangles, mopeds and bicycles were the favourites. Captain Stone had learned that the more unscrupulous seaman might attempt to smuggle cannabis or some other narcotic.

The following morning, at breakfast, only he, the Chief Engineer and Morgan sat together at his table. Captain Stone was parting meat from the bones of a pair of broiled kippers to disposable bone free mouthfuls of flesh. He posed to the company present the question as he nonchalantly worked away. 'I looked over the side last night and noticed that the marks were not visible, how can she possibly be so low in the water?' If the responsibility lay with him then, he had to come up with some answers.

It seemed to Captain Stone that Morgan awaited his question. He immediately spat out sourly, saying between mouthfuls of toast and marmalade with which he was finishing off his breakfast. 'Remember, Captain, the loading took place in the Indian dry season, with exceptional, if not freak sea conditions. We had high water temperature and high salinity within the Madras harbour. This would make the vessel buoyant in the extreme. Previous full-loads of jute that Mistral loaded in Madras, whilst I was Mate, did not put her below the marks, because she loaded in a wet season. You must have noticed the marks in the fresh water of the Humber. They would have looked significantly different.'

Morgan seemed pleased at his captain's plight, that he didn't know what was going on around him, seemed frozen in his chair. He waited until the captain had finished his kipper and was wiping his lips with his napkin when he pointed out. 'You of all people should remember that. There's a cargo plan hung in the ship's office with which you could have compared with previous loadings in Madras. The company have never complained that we were overloaded a trifle in the past. Might have lost cargoes had we been that fussy.'

In response, Captain Stone rather mumbled a belated knowledge of the previous occasions and felt unwilling to question him further.

He recognised that, while the boat was loading, alcohol influence would have played a part in disrupting his notion of events and this knowledge placed him in no position to ask questions that were more pertinent.

Chief Engineer Roddy McDonald nodded away in agreement, his eyes down as he spread a teaspoon of salt onto his porridge. Old Roddy loved to see discord in other departments.

Captain Stone felt happier he had an answer of sorts for the company superintendent. He also thought it would look strange and cause suspicion that he should be sounding fresh water tanks. That was normally the carpenter's job on the Minstral. He knew that, when docking had finally taken place, a time would arise when he could position himself adjacent to the sounding pipe while the carpenter sounded the tank, which he should do immediately after discharge had ceased for the day, and witness the results.

Two days later, on the morning tide, under a drizzle filled sky, the Minstral finally berthed alongside the jute berth in Hull docks. By 08-00 hours, she was a hive of activity. The dockside rumbled with the movement of the cranes along rail lines, positioning themselves adjacent to hatches. Dockers chatted as they took up their working positions. The removal of hatch tarpaulins and boards was the first job tackled to expose the cargo. Cargo nets descended above hatches on the ends of wire ropes, ready for dockers in the holds to fill, signalled the discharge had begun. Dockers, using lethal-looking, shiny metal hooks, began pulling bales of jute into them for hoisting ashore to a dockside shed.

Captain Stone was watching the unloading from an open cabin porthole. He wasn't interested: he'd seen it all before. He was on the lookout for the arrival of the Customs Officer and if he knew the person.

Old Billy Smith had officiated aboard his ship before. He was what crews knew as a 'two-ringer': a customs officer with two gold bands wrapped around his uniform sleeve. Ships' crews usually called them this because they didn't know their precise title within the customs service. Billy was long on experience and had always shown a generosity of allowances. Crews loved his presence as boarding officer. In the past, Billy had often, as a special favour to Captain

Stone, accompanied him in his taxi through the dock gates, police and customs on duty there, with his own briefcase filled with duty-free drink. Of course, Billy had his case stuffed with cigarettes and spirits, courtesy of the ship. Captain Stone knew he could talk to old Billy candidly. Billy would know what to do if he thought the circumstances warranted it. He hoped it was Billy.

At 09-00 hours, Captain Stone spotted the uniformed figure of customs officer Billy Smith weaving his way down the dockside, checking the unloading with an experienced eye and circuiting the busier quayside areas. He reached the steep gangway that afforded access to the after deck and ascended carefully, disappearing into the lower accommodation in the direction of the purser's office. Captain Stone waited contentedly whilst reading a morning newspaper. As he had gazed out over the dockers preparing Number 1 hatch, a considerate docker had thrust it through his porthole to him, as the first bale was being prepared for hoisting ashore. Billy would arrive at his door soon.

At 10-00 hours, a knock on his outer door heralded Billy's appearance. They shook hands as old friends. Captain Stone rang the bell to summon a steward. He ordered coffee, which the attentive steward left for, then returned and duly served. He mentioned to Billy that he was retiring. Billy confirmed that he was retiring at the end of the week and was moving to a villa in North Cyprus, there to see out his days in style with a good pension.

More than a year had elapsed since they last met. Normally, the Minstral was a hassle free ship, which was the way Billy liked it. However, something in Captain Stone's agitated manner told him it was not to be the case this time. And when he began his outpourings, he listened intently to Captain Stone's suspicions, noted his shakiness and guessed the Captain had been 'hitting the bottle' during the past voyage. Nevertheless, he could not dismiss what he heard out of hand. He couldn't afford to do that. Billy confirmed, putting Captain Stone at ease, that when Number 1 hatch had completely discharged, the 'black gang' would do their rummaging and investigate his claims.

Meanwhile Morgan superintended the unloading of the ship and attempted to keep it upright, as cargo disappeared ashore. This operation required the moving of ballast around the ship from tank to tank. Ballast in the case of the Minstral was oil or water, sometimes both, depending on the degree of list needing correction. This required the taking of tank soundings for the precise transfer of liquids between tanks. Captain Stone prepared himself to witness the taking of the sounding at Number 1 hatch.

At the end of the first day's unloading, the ship had a pronounced heel to port, which required correction. He decided to take a stroll along the forward deck just as the levelling operation began. He had stopped and was leaning over the starboard rail adjacent to Number 1 hatch, viewing the other vessels in the port, when he heard the carpenter approaching. From his position, he heard the top screwed from the sounding pipe of Number 1 fresh water tank and the rattle of the sounding cord's metal end rattling its way down the pipe as the carpenter lowered it to plumb the depth of water in the tank. If there were contraband in the tank, Morgan would not want any pumped in during the heeling operation. He turned as the metal end of the sounding line reappeared at deck level, noting with a grunt of satisfaction that it was dry. It was the only evidence he needed to convince himself of the righteousness of his thoughts and subsequent actions. That was it then: Morgan was using that tank for a smuggling operation.

The following afternoon at around 15-00 hours, Number 1 hatch emptied completely and a deck crew clambered beneath to sweep and clean out debris. At 15-15 hours, two dark blue mini-buses pulled up on the quayside and disgorged around twenty avid young men, who made up the latest compliment of the port 'black gang'. They seemed to know exactly where they wanted to search, some disappearing down the booby hatch of Number 1 hold with an assortment of large spanners, whilst others homed in on the Asian crew accommodation and the officer's cabins. This had all the portents of a major search.

Meanwhile, Morgan sat alone in his office pouring over his loading plan, whistling nonchalantly.

At 17-00 hours, Billy Smith again entered Captain Stone's cabin, greeting him with the statement that deeply shocked him. 'You're ships clean Captain. Number 1 water tank is empty because an inlet valve is broken. A repair is required before filling it again can begin.'

Billy was saying the wrong words. This could not be the case. He was so sure that Morgan was up to something. How could he be so wrong?

He was flabbergasted and sat down with a thump. Billy left and he reached for a gin bottle.

Four days later, the Mistral had completed her unloading. Captain Stone's replacement, Morgan, prepared himself for the short flit from his small cabin up the flight of stairs to the never before achieved luxuriousness of a Captain's cabin, with its bedroom and en-suite facilities.

He tried on his brand new uniform, complete with four gold bands of rank around its cuffs and his white topped steaming bonnet, complete with gold trimmings. These had arrived that morning from the local marine tailors. He swaggered in front of his mirror and commended himself on his smartness.

Peter Inigo Stone, recently retired, awaited the arrival of his taxi to take him to the train station. Billy Smith, who he figured to be suffering the ignominy of organising a wasted search, had not appeared to escort him through customs. He worried if the customs on duty at the dock gates would bother to search his cases and find his extra bottle of duty free gin.

At 16-00 hours, a black cab arrived at the gangway. Captain Stone rang for some assistance and a gaggle of Asian stewards appeared to assist with his baggage. No officer presented himself to wish him farewell. The Pist One was alone, once more.

From his bridge, Captain Morgan surveyed his domain and watched Captain Stone's departure. 'Silly bumbling, drunken old fool,' he mouthed loudly.

He remembered the night, just before Mistral anchored in Aden, when he'd visited Captain Stone in his cabin. He'd gone to inform him of the broken inlet valve discovered on Number 1 fresh water tank. It would take no water and it would remain empty when the water it contained the ship had used up. He found Captain Stone screaming at some perceived apparition sitting astride the foot of his bunk and was never sure if the message had sunk into his gin-befuddled brain.

Now, he could afford to smile contentedly, and mused: if Captain Stone, with all his poorly thought out suspicions, had only bothered to check the very first bale of jute landed ashore from Number 1 hatch. That one, he would have discovered, contained several hundred pounds of pure Afghani hashish, already sold on to dealers for a cool million untraceable pounds. He patted his back pocket symbolically, knowing that the result of the smuggling operation had already boosted his offshore bank balance. His shoreside collaborator, Billy 'two-ringer Smith', he mused, could also look forward to a good retirement for his part in the result.

First Tripper

A seagoing adventure

The party ended on a Friday night in October 1961. Twenty-one years-old then, I was sailing on the late-night tide aboard the Shaw Savill Line ship M.V. Coptic, as a first-trip 3rd electrician. From London's K.G.V Dock, Coptic was heading to discharge and load in Pacific Ocean ports. This was the biggest adventure of my young life, away from my family and the one-horse town of Annan, where I had spent all of my teens and my twentieth year.

I was also leaving behind the pubs around the docks, North Woolwich, East Ham and further afield, which I found were a source of fun, amusement and good for a few pints and often. Back then, the tipple was mainly Red Barrel and Double Diamond, which you don't see any more and Draught Bass: The Round House and the Royal Oak pubs, close by the docks. The Boleyn near the Hammers' football ground and The Green Man at Leytonstone also come to mind; all these pubs were meeting place and for all sorts. I even met two lads from my hometown, who were sailing with different companies to the one I had just joined.

I say the party ended because then the work began and it was relentless and dirty under taskmaster Chief Electrician, shall I call him John Girnley.

A hooley was blowing in the channel that Friday night. As a first tripper, I didn't know how prone I would be to seasickness. Sadly, I succumbed as we left the Thames and entered the stormy North Sea. It was a bit of a worry; especially how difficult I'd find getting my head off the pillow on Saturday morning at 7 am, to enter the engineroom and take a log of electric motor currents and to clean commutators with paint brush and rag.

Throughout the night, Coptic had ducked her bow into the swell with disturbing repetition, throwing in a few corkscrews as well, tossing pots and pans around the galley, the racket easily heard through the bulkhead of my adjoining cabin. That night was the only one during all my years at sea when I found sleeping in a narrow bunk a blessing. With a life jacket under one side of the mattress, making it rounded, it kept me secure during the night's wildest moments.

Improved conditions and larger cabins on later-built ships, three-quarter beds and en-suite facilities became the expected norm for officers and crew; though for some, conditions never got that good.

I did make the engineroom at 7am that Saturday. It was a half day for us leckies (electricians) and I managed to get through it, spending the afternoon in my bunk, with a book, keeping down any signs I might need to call out again Hughieeeeeeee.

I gained my sea legs quickly; I had no seasickness repeats throughout the five month twenty-three day voyage.

We had our first bond issue that weekend. The ration was a case of beer, a bottle of spirits, 200 fags and as much lime juice as you wanted. I recall the beer choice came in cans, either Barclay's Blue or Barclay's Red, one a lager the other export pale ale, and Green Can Guinness. Four Bells rum and Gordon's Gin seemed to be the favourite spirit tipple.

I had my first experience of cabin drinking that first Sunday morning, though I received no invite. After breakfast, the Chief Officer (C.O.) and Chief Refrigeration Engineer (C.R.E.) followed John Girnley into his cabin. An hour later, the two Chiefs left the cabin with huge grins on their reddened faces, closely followed by John with an empty gin bottle in his hand, which he hurled over the ships rail into the sea, then returned to his cabin to sleep.

I forget how many first trippers sailed that voyage. Certainly, there were three other Jocks sailing as first trip junior engineers. The CRE, the Second Fridge Engineer and a 3rd Engineer, and the 2nd leckie were also Jocks.

In the cooler weather of the Atlantic, Chief Electrician John Girnley made the maintenance of engine-room electrics his priority. Messrs. Swan, Hunter, and Wigham Richardson built the Coptic and launched her in 1928. Her engines, now running on borrowed time, spewed out oily fumes from orifices not designed for such emissions, which direct current electric motors and generators sucked into their interiors, causing sparking of commutators and the build up of oily grime around the armature, pole windings and brush gear. A strip down, clean with Armaclean then paint them, were the main maintenance requirements. An occasional burn out of a coil or armature necessitated a strip down and a change of parts.

Improved weather found the leckies on deck (where else), opening up winch controls and brakes. Most ports use cranes, but John impressed upon his squad the need for maintenance: we would be anchoring at Christmas Island (today known as Kiritimati) and off Apia, Samoa, using winches, and probably at some ports in New Zealand.

The island of Curacao was our only outward-bound bunkering port. Coptic pulled into a jetty, with the oil lines running along it, which stretched 100 yards out to sea from a bleak, uninhabited shore. The main town was the island's capital, Willemstad. Engineers who had previously called there, where at pains to explain the temptations for seamen, to all the agog first trippers, in the bag shanties (brothels) and bars festooning the quayside streets and stowed to the rafters with gorgeous girls. The winding up went well; the city was some miles away and not reachable in the time we were alongside, to the disappointment of the more adventurous. I recall being saddened.

A netted structure near the beach told of a safe swimming area, to which a few crew ambled and swam, cooling off any last vestiges of lurking, rampant thoughts.

A day later, we were ready to transit the Panama Canal. During the passage, a part of my duties was to keep a main-engine movement log, recording the time of any movement signalled from the bridge.

It was hot and sticky in the engine-room, but I worked the passage two hours on and two off with the 2nd leckie. I did see some of the canal; the only opportunity I had that trip of seeing the Coptic moving close to land. I'm sure old salts kidded a first-trip cadet into appearing on deck with a handful of carrots to feed to the mules: the mechanical ones that took ship's ropes and guided them safely through the lock system. Few of us first trippers were free from a 'piss take', generated by the more mature and knowing: perhaps the most important form of entertainment encountered in those satellite TV free days far out on the 'oggin'.

Short wave radio was a blessing, the BBC keeping us up-to-date with news from home. The Waldport Company had the contract to supply the ship with 16milimeter films, some quite modern, which the 2nd leckie showed on deck, to all the crew not working, after dark, of course, on a large screen strung up on the after mast.

At the Pacific end of the canal, Coptic tied up for the night to fill her fresh water tanks. It was an opportunity for us first trippers to have a run ashore. To the American Embassy was our first call, to exchange pounds to American Dollars, the currency used in Panama. We had hired a taxi to take us there and later to some bars. The taxi driver made a deal to take us bar hunting and to look after us, in what he explained was a dangerous city for white men. Of course, we believed him implicitly, even when we spotted him cruising along the same street twice whilst taking us to the first bar. These bars were the bag shanties of our imaginations and did, indeed, have some quite gorgeous, flimsily dressed hostesses who floated around us, there to satisfy the urgent desires of those seafarers in need.

Our first discharge port was an anchorage in London Roads, Christmas Island -- the Pacific island where Britain tested the Atomic Bomb. We had aboard NAAFI stores; winches discharged the Army's rations into a couple of Dukws: flat-bottomed, amphibious landing craft.

The waters around the island were like crystal and varieties of large fish circled Coptic; Manta rays and sharks, the biggest we saw, lost interest quickly before disappearing into deeper water. The carpenter had a leg of mutton fixed to a docker's hook and dangling in the water, but nothing fishy looked at it. A cargo cluster slung over the gangway bottom attracted smaller fish. Homemade harpoons were fashioned and some fun we had attempting to spear them. The captain, with a fishing line slung from the bridge deck, found the traditional kipper attached to his hook.

The British Government employed some Gilbert Islanders to skivvy on the island. I recall one who spoke good English came aboard. He asked a few of us where our homes were. When told Wales, he asked if we knew Mr Jones.

All officers had an invite to the officer's mess ashore, where we were dined and entertained in their bar, double g&ts costing 6 old pence, I recall.

A dukw was acting as a liberty boat. The C.O. berated the crew and threatened the logging of a day's pay for any members missing the boat back to Coptic that night. During the evening, in the bar, the C.O. went suddenly stiff with drink. Army personnel carted his prone body outside and placed beneath a coconut tree to sober up.

He and a greaser where the only passengers aboard the first dukw out next morning, the captain not recognising the wave he received on the bridge wing from the C.O. as the craft pulled alongside. The greaser was logged a day's pay; I guess the C.O. got just a quiet bollocking.

We carried an extra 3rd engineer, John Hourston, from The Orkneys, whose responsibility was to overhaul the generators. There always was one in bits during the outward-bound trip, readied to supply the extra electric load required to keep the refrigerated cargo cold or frozen during the trip back to the UK. John's hobby was model making, mainly building sailing craft and placing them into bottles. Very good he was at it. He even constructed a sailing ship from picked clean turkey breastbones. At Christmas Island, Army personnel presented the ship with sacks of large crayfish, which went down well for dinner one night. The 3rd even made a model from a crayfish shell; such was his expertise in the craft.

Years later, whilst on a cruise, I spoke with an ex captain of an Orkney ferry. He said a John Hourston was once a Chief Engineer onboard, but sadly, he had died of cancer. The Hourston surname is common to the north of Scotland and the Orkneys. Perhaps it was that skilled man, Big John. R.I.P

I visited Christmas Island in 2005, whilst cruising from Auckland back to the UK. Army presence had disappeared a few years previously. Most of the officer quarters were gone. Gilbert Islanders were using the Squaddie's huts. The children put on a song and dance for passengers, which was tuneful and colourful. I took a ride in a pickup to the Captain Cook Hotel, built on the site of the British Military base. On the way back to the village, which is Called London, I spotted the crushed-coral playing pitch were the Coptic crew had taken on a combined forces team at soccer. We lost by the single goal. The metal goalposts still stood, though rusty and bent; my best effort now was dribbling a coconut husk between a set.

Today, the Kiritimati group of islands and atolls have over 5000 inhabitants in scattered villages. Christmas Island is a beautiful atoll, though London smelled as if there was no sanitation available; the stink of raw sewage pervading, especially from around the back of the palm trees closest to the inhabited huts.

Apia, the Samoan capital, did not have a harbour then, though it does now and cruise ships tie up there. Coptic anchored a safe distance from the shore and Apia. Discharge commenced into barges. It was a short stopover. The junior ranks, given permission to go ashore during the daytime, streamed ashore after lunch. It seemed a generous gesture by heads of departments. It emerged later that the seniors had prior knowledge that local girls came out to play in the evening and planned their time ashore accordingly.

A memory I have of that night: awakened in the early hours by loud voices in the alleyway, I left my bunk to investigate. The C.R.E. had obviously enjoyed a great night ashore, had found a loving, compliant girl, had missed the last liberty boat back, and had co-opted a local with a catamaran for hire to take him out to the Coptic. The row was over the cost, the C.R.E. offering the local some bars of Sunlight Soap and pointing out that it wasn't ordinary soap, but contained the important, very expensive and rarely available-in-the-Pacific ingredient Lanolin. How is it possible that Samoans, in 1961, were unaware of the benefits of this, highly beneficial additive?

The permanent smile on the C.R.E's face next day was all it took for one to tell of a successful night womanising ashore.

The run from Samoa to Lautoka, Fiji, took about two days steaming: the old Coptic hardly ever got above 12 knots. I have little recall of the town back then, but did cruise into the port in 2004. I suppose I was amazed at the greenery of the island.

I found the Fijians a lovely, friendly people in 1961. I know they have their problems today, with immigration, etc. I would like to go back to Suva, just to visit. The few days Coptic discharged there were memorable. It rained quite often and cargo cluster lighting repairs on deck occupied me greatly.

I was bewitched in a nightclub by a Fijian girl who sang beautifully, 'Yellow bird, up high in banana tree, yellow bird, you sit all alone like me. A New Zealand Shipping Company passenger vessel docked. On board was Queen Salote of Tonga, on her way home from New Zealand. I recall hearing a large crowd of Fijian Islanders singing, 'Po Atarau', also known as 'Now is the hour, when we must say goodbye', as the ship left port, with the Queen waving from the rails. I also met a Fijian man with no arms, he losing them in a shark attack, selling postcards. All these were moving experiences, but for different reasons.

I was looking forward to my stay on the New Zealand coast. I had family there, in Auckland. Although Auckland wasn't one of our discharge ports, I was further delighted on hearing that it was a loading port and we could be alongside loading wool, mutton, cheese and butter for three weeks, and it covered the Christmas and New Year periods.

The Welsh family were from my mother's side. Ted had been a Cardiff police constable who couldn't see any prospects in that Force so emigrated, joining the New Zealand Force on his arrival there. When I first met him in his new country, he was Sergeant Welsh, who later made it to Superintendent, the prospects there as he had hoped.

A part of shipboard life in ports, in those days on the Kiwi and Aussie coasts, was for us officers to telephone nurses' homes and invite nurses to a ship's party. We always seemed to have duty free alcohol squirreled away for the events. Some of the nurses were very accommodating and stayed the night. Nurses tucked themselves tightly into the narrow bunks, alongside its normal occupant, with enthusiasm. A taxi in the morning to return the lodger to the nurse's home was usually the only cost involved but you never knew!

Of course, nightlife in New Zealand was difficult to find. One of the problems was the pubs closing at 6pm, every evening, and never opening on a Sunday. In those days, you could buy a carry out in the form of four-pint jars of lager, known to all as half gees (half gallons).

There was always the opportunity to 'Sly Grog', the term used to describe unofficial drinking that could be obtained after hours and which seemed to carry on without police interference. Rapping three times on the back door of licensed premises and asking for Joe, was usually enough to gain entry and enjoy an afterhours tipple, and to find the bar crowded with thirsty Kiwis and a number of crew from several ships.

The return voyage was a three-week battle across the Pacific to Panama; Coptic's engines requiring maintenance at sea caused many slowdowns and stoppages. Some days, especially when we neared the equator, the sea was like a mirror. Then we often saw dolphins cavorting in the distance. Spotting the Coptic, they'd veer towards her, to frolic and splash around her bow, before getting bored with that activity and shooting off into the distance. Flying fish were the most common marine creature seen; flying close to the sea for varying distances, then to disappear again with a splash. Occasionally, one would inexplicably soar higher and land on deck.

The voyage from Panama across the Caribbean and Atlantic followed much the same route, but in reverse However, in the Panama Canal, a clutch on the windlass disintegrated whilst picking up the anchor, which meant two things: seamen couldn't use the machine and we had to enter the Curacao capital, Willemstad, seeking repairs.

A Lloyd's surveyor came on board to assess the damage. His opinion was that as long as seamen could drop the anchor, he had no worries and we could sail on with the machine as it was. I assumed that had the seamen reason to drop the anchor, then they would need some other method of hoisting it back onboard.

Antwerp was our first discharge port. We tied up on the Scheldt River, after midnight, not too far from the city centre and the hoped-for nightlife. I think I had a run ashore, later that morning, to an all-night bar. It was all a part of the great adventure, but a disappointment, I recall.

Two days later, after another lengthy river passage, we tied up in Rotterdam. A part of the city, known as Chinatown, on the Katendrecht Peninsula, was the area in which we docked. It was a much more exciting place than Antwerp. The bars that weekend thronged with Dutch revellers, all out to enjoy the music of Dutch Swing College bands, many bars providing live music, some bands lining up in balcony-like structures, high up. The area looked old and well established, but today Chinatown has a new relocation in West Kruiskade, wherever that might be.

Two days later, again after a lengthy river passage, Coptic docked in Hamburg. My memory of all these discharge ports is sketchy, but Hamburg, with its window-shopping (Brothels) streets, where you could negotiate with a prostitute for a 'short time', if you were so inclined. I remember more fondly the Reeperbahn, the Zillertal bierhaus with its Bavarian oompah band and lederhosen-attired musicians. Mightily built fraus, carrying six litre-holding steins of bier in each hand, waited on the tables. The Zillertal bierhaus is the oldest tavern in the world with a capacity for 1200 drinkers.

Voyage end, London's K.G.V. Docks, the beginning and end of that and many other memorable voyages. Then it was back to the one-horse town of Annan for a spot of leave.

Cruise Games

The joker called out whilst leaning over the Starboard rail of Lido deck and pointing, 'That's the first flying fish seen this cruise.' Cruise ship Majestic had just left St Vincent, Capital of the Cape Verde Islands. Most of the voyage there had been through storm-force-10 seas and hurricane-strength winds; in the lea of the islands, the sea had calmed to an easy, low swell.

It was late in the afternoon and the sun had made a rare appearance. Mary, Molly and Milly, three octogenarian ladies, were out for a stroll and taking air on the lido deck. Linking arms as they gingerly passed the swimming pool, which was still slopping water, they were within earshot of the joker's cry.

Mary stopped jerkily in her tracks; Molly and Milly peeled militarily around her. In a line, they veered towards the rail, holding on to it with one hand each when they reached it. Following the direction of the spotter's outstretched finger, they trained their old eyes across the glinting sea, transformed, momentarily, from its greyish blue by the sun's late show. Alas the fish was gone, back beneath the waves, probably a bit less of a quiver now than when it first realised Majestic was on its tail.

The joker left his position and walked off, smirking wryly; the fish had been small, he had only seen its short glide over the waves for a second, but thought he'd raised the ladies' heartbeats a touch.

Spotting fictitious sea-life and watching the scramble for a viewing position on the ship's rails was a game that some cruisers played on others.

Mary turned to face the swimming pool, just as a corpulent and bald headed white man grabbed the pool ladder and eased himself from the water. 'Look girls, it's a white whale,' she said quickly

'Where,' Molly and Milly chorused, a hand to their foreheads giving their watering eyes shade, this time scanning the sea for a white blob.

Anecdotes

Table of Contents

An Eagle's View

I am but a distant blur suspended in the firmament, swooping, soaring hovering, circling, but mainly watching the colours changing upon the expanse of patchwork farmland beneath. The ripping wind tugs at my golden and brown feathers and plays havoc with my equilibrium, disrupting the important visual properties attributed to my species. A steady head and cool eyes the requirements necessary to ensure my mate and ravenous offspring eat.

Where is that bundle of fluff I seek leaping, bounding, scurrying from its camouflaged lair? Will the silver fish turn, flash in yonder expanse of blue water, its dark shadow appear in the shimmering stream, or the fat bird flight from the safety of its woods? Questions that need answers before the shadows lengthen and dappled moonbeams permeate the dark.

A coarse-woven nest of sticks, fleece and fur is our home, sited beyond yonder wood with its spiny green and brownish cones. There a craggy rock face, before the hill becomes mountain, where small gullies are still full with snow, a wide ledge provides support and shelter.

I see him now, a dot no more. He's standing tall with his long ears erect, this full-grown hare, on the loose and alone in the middle of a hay field newly mown. He lopes, stops and nibbles a repast of grass-- sustenance enough for him, ensuring strength for the night of dance and madcap activities for which he is famous, beneath tonight's late March moon, if he is lucky.

Circling high, I plot his direction and compute my flight-path. Shadows will do him no favours. I turn to face the setting sun that glistens red and appears half submerged in the loch ahead. I swoop low. I feel the rush. I see him tense, the whisper on the lips of death scenting. I arrow, talons outstretched, wing feathers spreading, braking to moderate that last moment of sudden, silent impact when claw clasps meaty saddle and scrawny neck. I feel the shock, the weight, the brief, useless struggling. The relief as life gives out.

Homeward bound I struggle gaining altitude over trees; the limp torso weighs heavily slung beneath, a dot that crossed before my eyes the starter for our teas.

Apres Le Defeat:
A Tale Of Supporter Dedication

After the match on Sunday, Lord Palmerston, walking down Terregles Street, Dumfries, and well into a swaggerless stride, approached Laurieknowe. There was little football traffic and the streets were quiet. Like the majority of the afternoon's attendance, he was contemplating Queen of the South's inept display.

A smell of smoked fags drew his attention to the cloaked figure suddenly appearing at his side and stride along with him. The figure was easily recognisable: its trademark short ponytail and a rusty scythe resting on one shoulder a dead giveaway. Suddenly, a rasping, Cumbrian voice boomed from the cloak's cowl, 'That was Gretna's second eleven you played today and you couldn't even beat them.'

The Lord turned to face the voice as Devorgilla Bridge hove into view, but the cloaked figure had disappeared, leaving behind the aroma of a full ashtray. Although he was sick and tired of the trash served up on the pitch, the Lord was unable to accept this rant against his heroes. He raced on to the bridge, selected the first parapet, leapt and hurtled down into the deep, swift flowing, unforgiving waters beneath. A slight misjudgement saved him and he landed on six alcoholics with sunburnt faces, sitting on the Whitesands nursing cans of Carlseberg Special.

Dusting himself down, he headed for The White Hart Hotel. Here, punters saw him standing tall, on a bar table, holding a length of rope with a perfectly-spliced hangman's noose and knot at one end. The bar having a low ceiling, he was unable to find a suitable fixing point from which to hang himself. Leaping from the table, delicately onto tiptoes, he left the Hart shouting 'I'll no' be back until the roof's raised.'

Leaving The White Hart, the Lord entered a nearby Chinese restaurant and asked for a dog sandwich. A customer there, fearing the Lord was out to end himself, and noting a chef race from the kitchen with a cleaver, ushered the Lord out into the High Street.

I found him there shortly after that incident. Six heavy-set polis and a medical team attended the scene. One polis was holding each limb of the writhing Lord, while the other two prepared the straitjacket. The Lord was raving and his lips were spittle-flecked. Growling like an imminent volcanic eruption, with heavy emphasis on the GR…, he would then explode with a violent shout of ETNA.

A medic eventually rammed a phial of horse anaesthetic into the Lord's butt, which quietened him considerably, but only for a short time, as his love for the Queens will never die.

I saw him later as he recovered in an emergency ward. Sitting up and tucking into a yard of Cumberland sausage, he looked is old self.

He'll be back at Palmerston Park on Wednesday night. He's short of 'Ayr on a G-string' to serenade the opposition! Bring your old 78 along, if you have it.

Some Thoughts On Racehorse Betting

The closest I came to equines in the 1940s, when I was growing up in a Dumfriesshire village, was Clydesdales and a donkey. Both had a use at the local farm; the horses yoked to ploughs and carts, the donkey coming into use when a young relation of the farmer arrived each summer holidays. The cuddy, as we villagers knew donkeys, the farmer hitched to a buggy and all the village kids had a hurl on it around the country lanes.

Gambling was no big issue then. The local estate gamekeeper occasionally received a tip from one of his boss's landed friends. When the information was imminent, the gamekeeper took a homing pigeon with him to work, which he released for home with the tip, written down on a piece of fag packet, no doubt, attached to a leg. An accomplice posted the bet to a city bookmaker, there being no village public telephones or another way to bet in those unenlightened days.

I cannot recall any villagers, privy to the information received this way, who ever made fortunes.

However, I do know of a person who did make a few bob from horseracing some years later. But he had to circumvent the bookmaker's secure device to do it. All are long gone now so it's safe to tell the tale.

In those days, Bookmakers entrusted their runners with a 'clock and bag'. The bag to put the bets in, the clock mechanism to seal the bag and start the hidden clock, thus registering that the runner had sealed the bag into the mechanism before racing began that day.

The runner discovered that, by gently prising open both sections of the clock mechanism, using matchsticks, mainly, the clock, with a little shake, could be started at anytime, thus enabling the insertion of a winning bet before sealing the bag into the clock mechanism. The bookmaker never suspected that the runner had written out the bet long after the running of the race. The runner made his beer money this way, was never greedy, allowing the swill and the swindle to endure for a number of years.

There was one instance when the runner thought the bookmaker had twigged his racket: he changed the clock mechanism to a foolproof, unfiddleable appliance.

However, the runner found a way around this. He discovered a tiny hole in the bag. It was never large enough to be noticeable, nor could it be. The runner used this to his advantage to win. He would write the name of a horse on a slip and position it inside the bag, clipped on the outside so it didn't move. The space just in front of the horse's name the runner aligned with the hole. If the horse won, there was just room for the runner to scribble £1 win, if it lost, the runner only placed a10p bet to win, then shake the bag so the slip didn't stand out from the others.

Then the bookmaker reverted to the original 'clock and bag'.

Bookies still win, no matter what.

As the author of this piece, I can say I like a small bet, but I've found no system as good as the runner's.

The Parrot Distressed By My Grandson Came Calling

It was a sultry night indoors in uptown Annan. The house windows I left ajar, inviting in any cooling breeze calling by.

Living where I do, in a safe heaven, it did not incur to me that an intruder would enter my home overnight, but one did.

Imagine my surprise, whilst I prepared an early-morning brew, to hear a melodious whistling and on searching its source find, half-hidden amongst some suspended greenery in the dining room, this waif-of-the-feather. Settled and seemingly unruffled amidst the foliage was this pretty, African Grey parrot.

I approached the parrot carefully, not wanting to cause it alarm; but alarmed I was when I saw the condition of this gentle, soft natured bird. Displaying no hawkishness or raptor qualities, it was someone's pet and somebody had attacked it.

A crescent-shaped weal, visible beneath head feathers, and a scattering of gristly bits sticking to its under-pruned plumage, suggested someone had tossed a tin of dog food at this lovely bird and that it had struck its target a glancing blow, causing distress and injury; if not too much to the body, had the experience damaged the bird's mind?

Who could do this to such a lovely creature?

I offered a finger, which was immediately accepted. The parrot hopped on and perched. Now I know some African Greys have a vocabulary of more than 600 words, a few more than some people I know have, but what this parrot began saying to me did not make any sense. 'Dratsab yuG,' meant nothing to me. Neither did, 'em evol t'nseod yuG.'

As the morning progressed, I began to make more sense of the utterances: it was talking backwards, obviously disorientated by the head blow.

The parrot and owner are reunited, but I believe a chilly relationship still exists between the thrower and my lovely, overnight visitor.

Indian Street Practitioners

A Personal View

I have personally witnessed scores of Indian Ear Cleaning practitioners working at their profession, as the year nears its end, on the annual, festive cleaning of the lugholes of the hearing-impaired-by-dust-and-wax patients and there are queues of them.

Quite obviously, India being a dustbowl and the Asian Indian the best producers of earwax on that continent, there's sackloads of work on the pavements of Mumbai, where this picture was taken.

However, as I watched it became apparent that these executors of the lughole cleanout had a secret: they could clean out both ears from one side of the head. Unbelievable, I know, but it seems ancient lughole-cleaning gurus taught their protégée artisans the location of the secret tunnel running between the ear canals of each lughole. Now that's productivity in my book and why industry on the Indian continent is leaving us behind in so many ways.

Another little-known Indian-street consultant is the 'Boil Sucker'. This is a more ancient and needful art, performed only by men. The boil can be a painful plague to the skins of us all, but the Asian Indian suffers most. I have also seen boil suckers in action; indeed, it's a gut-wrenching sight to behold.

Typically, the boil sucker uses a hollowed out length of bamboo to perform the operation. The boil sucker requests the patient to reveal the location of the boil, sensitive areas included. To jog your memory to a boil's appearance: it has a red and bluish base, very painful looking and intensely so to the touch, with a crimson, volcanic stack, upon which rests the yellow, Korma-coloured, suppurating tip not quite ready to erupt.

The boil located and sized, the boil sucker selects a bamboo pipe with a suitable inner diameter from an array of such instruments suitable for treating anything from a zit to the dreaded, double-headed carbuncle.

At this point, the boils sucker offers the boil bearer the opportunity to take, for a small extra fee, a piece of seasoned teak to grip between teeth whilst the procedure takes place. Few sufferers refuse this offer.

The teak placed and gripped solidly between teeth is the cue for the process to begin. The boil sucker places the bamboo tube over the boil, then presses it downwards to ensure a good seal. The patient screams, slavers fly from his lips. Teeth crunch onto the teak. Sweat flows from the brows of both the boil sucker and the patient.

The boils sucker places the other end of the bamboo tube into his mouth. His lips closing about the tube, much in the manner a Venus flytrap plant collapses around its victim. He breathes several times through his nostrils. He evacuates his lungs. His ribcage shrinks to half its original size.

His cheeks sink inwards as the evacuation of the boil commences. The opposite inner linings of his mouth touch. The bamboo tube begins to creak as the vacuum increases. Teeth crumble in the boil-bearer's head as both gums attempt to meet at teak centre.

One minute into the procedure and the boil sucker's eyes have enlarged, are forcing out of their sockets. The boil-bearer has become unconscious, his teeth littering the pavement like a scattering of shattered, curry-stained pearls. The boil is now two-thirds of the way up the bamboo tube, inexorably on its way out the top.

Then there is a sound, much like that of an elephant removing a foot from quicksand and the boil sucker's head rocks backwards, the bamboo pipe, released from its suction, leaps from the operation site.

As the boil sucker turns his head looking for his next patient, he spits the contents of the boil into the gutter, where hungry vermin and vultures fight over it. Stretcher-bearers, always on standby, cart the patient away to the recovery suite, a swept clean pavement around the corner.

I saw it, I swear.

Thoughts On The Scottish Referendum

A Scottish think-tank with the title 'Plughole-here-we-come under Salmondisation', and known by the acronym PUS, has been making some forthright and hard-hitting predictions, whilst focusing on Scottish resident's futures, supposing (God willing there's not) there's an independent Scotland after 2014.

The think-tank suggests that the generated mammon Salmond and Co prophesy will accrue in the years following their guessed at independence vote is fanciful, will never happen, and will require all Scottish residents to own an unpaid slave, who will need to find lucrative employment to support his owner. The downside of the slave-ownership will be the rampant increase in immigration, mainly from Eastern Europe and the Indian sub-continent, and the transformation of the streets of all major towns and cities. The picture is what PUS foretells of what a Glasgow Street junction will look like shortly after 2014.

On the other hand, they say, if the wealth promised by Salmondisation doesn't materialize, by magic wand or from copying Icelandic and Irish Republic successes, as predicted by Salmond, himself, the junction will *still* resemble the photograph as poverty strikes a population driven to cheaper means of travel, food and housing.

Already such Indian family names decorate, in Hindi, Urdu and any of the fifteen-hundred other languages spoken by Indian sub-continent inhabitants, shop and restaurant frontages in all areas of Scottish towns and cities.

Meaningful Old Scottish Words

Some wonderful, old Scottish words out there are still meaningful today. Glaikit is one of them and I know Scots still use the word in its proper sense. According to my dictionary of Scottish words, it means thoughtless, stupid, irresponsible, full of pranks and tricks, foolish and of low intelligence. We will know people who have all of these traits, even to having a glaikit look on their coupons (faces).

The other interesting word still in common usage north of the Border is Sleekit. My dictionary tells me it means smooth, oily, fawning, cunning, self-seeking wheedling, unctuous and ingratiating.

Robert Burns used the word in his poem 'Ode to a Mouse'; not to describe the parlous state of the mouse unearthed from its winter home by his plough, but of the gloss on its fur.

Today, glaikit might not fit everyone's view of Scottish politicians; after all, most will have had a great education, even if their coupons don't mirror that fact, but just that they've been somewhat well fed. In my opinion, sleekit certainly does fit those who would attempt to 'pull the wool' over Scottish eyes, even if it is glossy, thinking us glaikit, with respect to independence. Who is the most unctuous, oily, fawning, cunning self-seeking wheedling and ingratiating party leader amongst them?

I think we know that!

Nuff said.

History Lesson

The main shopping street in my hometown climbs steeply for a mile and a half: that's why it looks shagged out. On a weathered, sandstone plinth, marking the high-end of the street, a huge, bronze statue of an antlered stag stands rampant, its nostrils flaring, its eyes glaring madly. Beneath the bridge at the lower end of the street, the river flows between grassy banks.

Credulous yesteryear townsfolk believed that the stag clambered down from its plinth every midnight, pranced down the street to the river, had a sniff around and a piddle there, then returned to the plinth. Early town scrolls suggest this myth was the main factor motivating those old townies to name the thoroughfare, Buck Loo Street.

By all accounts, a local Duke changed the spelling to Buccleuch.

Chance Meeting On Buck Loo (Buccleuch) Street

On the Friday morning of the week, looking for clothing before shipping out on a cruise, I walked along Buchleuch Street. And on the pavement, outside the draper's-department doorway of the large store to which I was heading, I spotted an erstwhile mate of mine: 'Wee Jock Laurie'. Jock was standing stooped, bawling his eyes out, surrounded by a pool of his own blood. Droplets from a haemorrhage, falling steadily from beneath his flowing raincoat, were spreading the pool and sending ripples across its surface. Other shoppers just passed by this ragged, dishevelled and obviously distressed, horizontally challenged man, averting their eyes.

They were uncaring people: Jock was an old mate who had often lent me the price of a pint of beer when I was skint. I just had to act. And being outside a prestigious store, I began by asking genteelly, 'What in heaven's name's the matter?' Taking a step back after my enquiry, I tried to assess Jock's problem for myself.

'I've caught my foreskin up in my zip,' he told me between the heart wrenching sobs and the drawn-out, high-pitched squeals he let out when he inched his body towards the erect position and looked up at me, 'and the agony's killing me.'

Jock was ghostly white, blue of lips and sweat flowed freely from his brow; he was displaying the classic symptoms of shock.

Sensing he was unable to help himself and that he might bleed to death, I rushed through the draper's department swing doors, throwing them back to their stops, and entered the store, resolved to seek help.

Hurriedly, I skirted displays of gent's shirts, suits and dinner jackets and found the nearest counter. A tall, lanky girl, standing poised at the till, was dressed in an apron of the establishment. She smiled readily in my direction and revealed through over-rouged lips an empty space once filled by an upper-front tooth.

Focusing on the toothless gap, images of the entrance to Fingal's Cave sprung into my mind. My thoughts also strayed to the gap's uses: like gripping a pickled onion, holding, rotating and stripping it layer by layer.

But she displayed the eagerness of the first-day shop assistant and her willingness to serve me was clear. 'Quick,' I ejaculated, 'can you give me something with which I can dress a dickhead?'

'Sorry, I tried but I cannot raise any help for you in there,' I said to Jock, as I appeared in front of him wearing a Batman outfit.

A Letter To A Non Lover Of Dogs

SPAT HOUSE
CURZON BOULEVARD
DOGSBURY ON SEA

Dear Cur,

S.P.A.T, the Society for the Preservation of Animal's Testicles, are aware of your intention to neuter your mutt. In our opinion, only a heartless owner, having followed in the wake of their faithful, knowing friend, having viewed those almond-shaped pods of canine fertility, swinging back and forth and gently line astern, like sleek craft rolling gently on a glassy sea, would have those goolies whipped off.

As the protector of all animal testicles for S.P.A.T., I must urgently warn you of the unforeseen costs: the six well-known tribulations that you will endure after subjecting your mutt to this irreversible, surgical procedure.

Firstly, howling his head off whilst you drag him along the street to Castration Alley, you will realise a number of things. Your mutt knows the address to which you're taking him, *he* knows who practices there and the outcome of such appointments, that *he* will be less two appendages when he returns home and that this fact is etched into the wary-side-of-the-brain of every male of the species,.

Secondly, veterinary science suggests that neutered dogs' diets drastically change; they become addicted to junk foods, become gross, lazy and fart continuously, having suddenly developed a taste for pickled eggs, onions both pickled and fried, smoky-bacon flavoured crisps, baked beans, Brussels sprouts, raw turnips, sulphur tablets and bowls of draught Guinness and Draft Bass.

113

Thirdly, owners of neutered dogs have tried many cures for their mutt's appalling anal flatulence. Many have discovered the only solution is a liberal application of Preparation H, the human haemorrhoid treatment. Careful insertion of the unction high into the dog's anus on the end of the index finger soothes significantly their dog's woopsy-extruders as it swiftly metamorphoses into a shape similar to the end of a sausage roll, after suddenly having to pass rapidly moving and unusually high quantities of methane.

Fourthly, owners of these altered beasts have found to their cost the inflated price of Bob Martin's Warfarin suppositories. This costly product they have also inserted into their dogs' anuses, in the misguided belief that rats had somehow breached the sphincter muscle and had remained there even after death.

Fifthly, this diet has resulted in shop and inn owners ejecting many poor, demented beasts from the vicinity of other human beings, under clouds of their own creation.

Sixthly, this seems a very high price to pay to curtail the amorous activities of any Charlie, Rover, Spot, Jack, Messi or Fido.

Yours Courteously,

Ivor Muttley

A Letter From Diddy Fuels To An Idiot

THE DIDDYUNIT
GLENARM ROAD
MAXWELLTOWN
DUMFRIES
DG6 9AU

Dear Sir,

We at DIDDY FUELS pride ourselves at being 'on the ball', when it comes to rectifying diddy-motorists' howlers. We also pride ourselves with our abilities to create products of mind-blowing potential for the alleviation of such diddy motorists' complications.

In the last six months, you will obviously be so annoyed to hear, you were the only motorist outside County Kerry to have made the 'faux pas' of mistaking petrol for diesel, and refilling your tank wrongly with one or the other of the these products.

We would not expect lorry drivers or seasoned travellers to make such a mistake, or anyone who is well-read, has good eyesight and has been educated to even a lowly standard.

However, help is at hand for all diddies out there.

Let me introduce our innovative product, 'ANTIDIDDY'.

ANTIDIDDY is a product that motorist diddies can add to a fuel tank, erroneously containing a mixture of petrol and diesel. It does not matter what product was in the tank first, which might surprise you, as well as County Kerry motorists. Therefore, there is no need to worry if you wrongly put petrol into a diesel tank, or vice versa.

ANTIDIDDY removes an electron from the valency of both fuels' atomic structures, rendering the mixture suitable for ignition in both diesel and petrol engines. Simple!

This is a much more ingenious and more cost effective method of dealing with this problem than having the vehicle towed into a garage to be charged £80+VAT, an hour, for the privilege.

Problems can arise when starting an engine with the ANTIDIDDY-treated fuel mix. It may take several engine turns before the engine recognises the new fuel, but it will. You should, next time you fill up, take time to recognise the difference in fuels.

Ivor Diddy

Creating A Character In A Monologue

Mother told me I was 9 pounds fourteen ounces at birth. I often heard her brag I was the largest baby born in Glasgow during the sixties. My father thought feeding me would make too much of a dent in his booze money and buggered off. I don't remember him and I won't be looking for him now. Mother worked hard after he left home. She looked after me well and brought me up with a work ethic. Now I work long hours running my own mini-cab company. I've had an offer from a rival to sell. What the rival doesn't know is that I'll be looking to buy them him out inside five years. I'm looking after my mother now; arthritis is crippling her and she needs constant assistance. That I have to provide the assistance is a responsibility that doesn't hassle me. But I hate seeing her in pain.

Growing up in Govan in the sixties was growing up poverty stricken. There were some other annoyances too. I ask you, who wants the handle Fatso for the whole of their childhood?

Some of those wee wide boys could be brutal and scathing towards their more unfortunate looking counterparts. The fact that I was bright at school, had a jolly face, blonde hair, and steely blue eyes mattered for nothing to them. In Govan, if you looked like Humpty Dumpty the wee wide boys treated you like Humpty Dumpty. They bounced me from more structures than walls they did. A nudge from a tenement landing was the wee wide boys' favourite pastime. Yours truly always bounced a bit higher than others did for their sadistic enjoyment.

Then at puberty, things changed. My height increased and at fifteen years of age, I was six feet tall. The puppy fat dropped off me and rippling muscle replaced it. My build was strapping, my chest was like a barrel, forty-six inches around. My stomach muscles showed a well pronounced six-pack and the lassies said I had a nice arse. The nickname suddenly changed from Fatso to 'The Big Yin' and for the first time in my life, I was in demand from more than just my mother.

By the time I was sixteen years of age every lassie in Govan wanted me to walk her out. The lassies loved me for my Govan repartee, my good looks, and my unusually blue eyes. Dressed in T-shirts, jeans and Adidas trainers, my stomach muscles showing taut, I was a regular Adonis, the cock of the walk.

The wee wide boys were now giving yours truly a wide berth. I see some of them at the fitba on Saturdays. Most of them turned out to be wasters, filling themselves with the swally and staggering around blootered. But I never went after them to inflict 'pay back'. Revenge was something I was well capable of exacting, but that's not my way. Mother brought me up to respect individuals for all their shortcomings and I still do. And I've never thought that giving up my seat on a bus so an elderly person can sit down made me look soft.

I'm on the lookout now for a girl like my mother was. Looks will come second. If she's honest, hard working, and I can see beauty behind her eyes, I'll love her forever. Together, we'll raise a family. I'd like all boys, but girls will be just as loved in my house. I'll buy a couple of greyhounds and run them at the local tracks as a hobby. I'll keep myself fit walking them. There will be no weight gain for me and I'll pass on the passion I found for bodily fitness to my children. I won't have my bairns thought of as Humpty Dumpties. I went through enough of that.

The Annals Of The Annan Mince Front, Other Spoofs and lies

Annan Mince Front 'American Wild West' Discoveries

The Annan Mince Front Historians, seeking the earliest mentions of mince in the annals of the 'American Wild West', discovered some interesting facts, echoes of which we might hear in present day shops.

Amongst the Wampum, the useless other than for adornment whelk shells and the thought-sacred coloured beads, peddled by American settlers to the native Indians, mainly the Comincehao Tribe, was poor quality buffalo meat.

Adolph Fleischwolf, a settler from Germany, changed this. He brought with him to the emerging USA the first commercially-viable mincer. Immediately, the meat mangler swept the need for chewing the tough animal protein to extract its nourishment under the log table and out of the tepee door. Now settlers and Indians could slurp buffalo meat straight from a spoon, like mommy's and gaho's jam.

One will recall that early western films, depicting the lives of the first settlers and the Indian tribes, showed them with broken or stumpy teeth, the result of sustained chewing on the almost inedible, gristly buffalo meat.

Later westerns showed one disadvantage of buffalo-mince eating: the film's cowboy heroes had wide, super-white, toothy grins. However, all had to wear broad-rimmed Stetsons to keep the sun from reflecting off the shiny molars, which could alert Indian war parties to their presence.

Today, in our butcheries, when a Chinese person shops and asks for wam pum mince, the butcher will, with the tact and benign air of a Mr Jones of Dad's Army type, say that will be just under a half kilo, Mr Wong.

A Bulletin On A Future Event

FLADEHOP, aka the Flogging A Dead Horse Party, have invited the A.M.F to procure mince in quality, but not quantity, for their 'Bonfire of the White Paper' night.

In darkness, after the result is known on the 18th of September 2014, the unsold 10000 or so copies of the greatest Scottish fairy story ever told, but never read, will send the black smoke of capitulation into the starlit skies above recently-reek-free Auld Reekie.

Oleaginous, Scottish, political-fantasist, the writer Eckie McGreasy, and his cohorts, penned the failed tome, which amassed some 650 transparently unbelievable pages.

Eckie will ignite the total five million, eight-hundred thousand and five hundred or so pages, using a smouldering peat clump, at the commencement of the cheerless cremation wake, held on the Spanish lawn of the Holyrood Parliament.

The sombre vigil, when attendees consume our organically-sourced mince and Ayrshire-potato mash, will fire up shortly after the official announcement of FLADEHOP'S trouncing in next year's separation referendum and the necessary TV appearances, but not before the smoke from the pyre has quickly risen above the height of wee Eckie.

We at the A.M.F anticipate our quality mince fetching full-belly joyfulness to most gatherings. At this, we expect to see the glum, the broken-hearted, hearing attendees wailing sillily in a language akin to Swahili and weeping profusely into sodden tissues, others making the mournful sounds of the rutting gnu and looking weirdly woebegone, the wretched throng ready to plunge from castle embattlements in dizzying displays of vanquishment.

FLADEHOP will have achieved something, though: Auld Reekie had remained smokeless for many years until the black cloud..................

We at the A.M.F do not apologise for being firmly entrenched in the NO camp.

Annan Mince Front Pronouncement On Burger Contamination

According to troubling information revealed by British Government meat inspectors yesterday, it's obvious that several supermarket chains have not been reading Annan Mince Front warnings and guidelines about the additives with which some beef burger manufacturers can adulterate their product.

The meat inspectors report that, in some case, beef-burgers were 29% horse with a smidgen of pig, probably the squeal, thrown into the mixture for added taste.

In our opinion, proper policing of burger-recipe contents by staff trained for the purpose is required, to spot the difference between cattle, horses and pigs. City-folk have proved unsuitable for such positions.

Modern abattoirs work on the continuous-throughput method: the cattle, pigs or horses arrive in cattle floats at one end of the processing plant. In the pens, there's usually a great roaring and visible arousal from bulls when they get a whiff of cow urine, which is full of tantalizing pheromones, released in streams, probably through fear of impending death.

The animal enters the plant, is killed with a bolt to the cranium, hung up by the hind legs and gutted, the head and skin removed, then another operative will hack the spine from tail to neck, splitting the carcass down the middle.

After this point, the carcasses are steadily advancing through the plant on an overhead conveyor system, but operatives should still be able to identify which type of animal is passing by.

As the roundabout carries the split carcass of a cow, bull, bullock from base to base, butchers slice off the various joint, the good cuts for the steak market, stewing steak types and steak mince. Trimmings and bone scraping provide for inferior beef mince and burger production. It's the same system of butchery with the horse or pig.

We at the A.M.F have no idea into what joints butchers might slice a horse. Certainly, a horse chop would be too large for my normal plate size, the T-bone totally out of the question. Americans pray before every meal, which can be up to eighteen times a day. In our view, eating horse T-bones could reduce their prayer time considerably.

We at the A.M.F consider that beef mince should be entirely beef mince and burger makers should never pollute it with cheap, other-animal meat.

Annan Mince Front Assisting At The Royal Birth

Yesterday, there was a pregnant silence emanating from the disused Kingdom hall, a building of many doors, once the training centre for Jehovah's Witnesses, but now the head office of different, unwelcome knockers: the mince front for Annan.

We leaked early in the afternoon, what later became widely reported, that a high ranking government official had requested the presence of the Grand Master Wizard Collop of the Annan Mince Front at the birthing suite in the Linoleum Wing of St Mary's Hospital, Praed St, Paddington, London W2 1NY.

A well-known establishment woman, who wished to remain anonymous, had developed the munchies and craved a meal of minced beef, dumplings, tattles, with a tian of carrot, turnip and haggis accompaniment, following her exertions to deliver the baby who had generated huge interest across an expectant Mother Earth.

A lightening dash by Virgin and Tube took me there. I listened to requirements and provided the recipe 'Viande hachée a la Ecosse', a truly Scottish recipe, with just a soupcon of garlic to tantalise the taste buds, and a dish favoured by Bonnie Prince Charlie, on his return from exile in France.

Being of blue blood, common or English mince was not considered regal enough for this woman; therefore, only Scottish ingredients, as the woman had enjoyed during her university days, in pies and whilst holidaying at a prestigious, Perthshire castle, were considered suitably tasty and nourishing after the ordeal of giving birth.

However, whilst lips were smacking, the attending family devouring the exquisite food, they bestowed credit for its preparation and selection of the meat cut from which the mince was ground on yours truly and discussed, ad nauseam, the suitability of names for the boy child: **A**lexander, **M**alcolm and **F**rank being amongst the favourites.

The **A.M.F** were happy to assist bring about a fitting conclusion to this perfect day.

Annan Mince Front Delegation Visits Tromso

The delegation found Tromso is the 'City of Midnight Fun' as claimed in touristy brochures featuring the Norwegian town. However, their cuisine is questionable. Mincaloo, a stew made from dried reindeer mince tops the menu in many Sami bistros. Putemince, featured on the menus of both haut cuisine and greasy finger restaurants. This odd dish, which none of the delegation ordered, has an even stranger preparation:

Water infused with caustic soda and potash imported from the Dead Sea expands dried mince to a jellied consistency when mixed together. Placing it beneath the raging waters of a high waterfall for many days, removes the chemicals. Traditionally, Sami's serve mincaloo with bacon, peas and spuds. Sounds a bit like potted head to me.

Police Commander Knut Nepehodet met the Annan Mince Front delegation on their recent visit to Norway. Knut guided us through the pitfalls evident if believing all of the country's folklore. Examples: There are no Trolls. But vertically challenged hirsute types are sometimes mistaken for this imaginary creature. Norwegians don't poach reindeer. The meat is a tough, but tenderer when roasted in an oven on Norwegian Sector North Sea Gas, Mark7, sixty minutes per kilo.

We discovered that the reindeer is many Norwegian's daily staple, a fillet mignon roast the favourite, not only of the northern-dwelling Sami people. Domesticating an animal is easy. The chosen one, known by Norwegians as "Den yuletide slaktingen", "the Christmas slaughter", is chosen in springtime and encouraged to dwell contentedly in the garden of householder; where, without too much bullying or training, it will become a much-loved "children's pet". The keeper feeds it dried seaweed to eliminate the flavours of tundra mosses and lichens and to induce the favoured "Viking Taste".

With plenty of time for hanging before Christmas feasting and festivities, the tamed animal will receive the "order of the bullet",

"Rekkefølgen av kulen" in Norwegian, the lead crisply despatched into the animal's cranium from short range, hastening death, tenderer, less stringy meat the result.

The carcass will provide meat cuts and mince for the cold, dark and dreary winter months ahead, the fur a warm overcoat, the head and antlers a trophy to display proudly above the hearth and for a game of hoopla. The guts, washed in the glacial waters of a nearby stream, Norwegians will use to make local sausage varieties.

Children will learn of the Christmas names traditionally given to these animal types whilst witnessing the annual slaughter. Adults will chant, just to see their kids blubber: Bambi, Rudolph, Dasher, Dancer, have gone Prancer, Vixen, Doner and Blitzen have gone too,

Annan Mince Front's Thoughts On Same Sex Marriages

Legislation mooted by the government to allow same sex marriages in church, irks the sensitivities of all brethren of the Annan Mince Front. Let us be clear on this subject: we stand for mince, not for mincing.

As universal upholders of mince standards, we find it somewhat sad that two men will go mincing together. Whether it happens as they skip down the aisle, buttocks Vaselined and ready, hand-in-hand, towards the matrimonial obligations that a pseudo-straight, chocolate speedway rider, bishop-bashing, white-collared type will place upon them, or in some seedy, gay haunt infested with other shirttaillifters, turd burglars and helmet munchers, we think it's still more masculine to share a pan of manly mince.

The upshot of any man-on-man marriage must include larger, man-sized rings, a natural conclusion to the continuing, sphincter expanding characteristics of the relationship and not of finger thicknesses. Perhaps our phoney, preposterous, discredited rivals the mince front for Annan can advise such couples on a fatty, inferior mince to grease and ease the passages of them towards a happy, anally-less-painful future together.

However, there's hope. Gays might find it much easier to push shite up a hill without using a wheelbarrow, as the Tories do getting this law past the rump of heterosexual British people.

Annan Mince Front Grand Tour Of Northern Iberia

Last week, Past Grand Wizard Collops of the Annan Mince Front, at our Mincing Lane Lodge, performed the regular, secret ritual and undertook their duty to install me to the throne of Grand Wizard of the Ancient Collop. My remit for Annan Mince Front is as overseer of mince preparation, fat reduction techniques, organic-additive selection and sourcing novelty-value catering accessories, worldwide and beyond. The position extends ahead for one lunar year.

Since that deep and thought-provoking moment of initiation into high office, I have been quick to visit pastures new: the Northern Spanish town of Al Fellover, the latest place.

This was a necessary visit. The cultured citizens of this enlightened town have a well-organised and highly respected Mince Front. Al Fellover Front's Grand Wizards from the past, together with the present incumbent, made me welcome and shared with me some of their most sought-after secrets.

I learned that an interesting aspect of the mince culture in this region of Spain is the packaging and the ease of accessing the product after cooking in oil, garlic, rosemary and thyme, a touch of mint and tomato paste, with a shot of Tabasco for those with an adventurous palate. Also, that trained envelopers seal the succulent meatiness within an intriguingly-shaped, wax shell.

To sup mince as we do is like taking mother's milk, no other utensil required, delegates told me.

Quickly, I learned of the packaging's simplicity and uniqueness. Here we see a photograph of the casings, known to Al Felloverians as (carne picada mamaria): mince mamaries, here, seen sitting alongside some Al Fellover (queso) cheese products in a local market.

I think this remarkable invention only God could have thought of previously. It also seems Saint Simon Da Costa, patron saint of above-waistline, frontal, feminine appendages, favoured these shapes in the distant past.

I was eager and on standby to sup mince this way for the first time. Alas, my wife, who had travelled with me, was hostile to my sampling. Accessing and releasing the flavoursome product required a turning, tweaking motion between a finger and thumb of one hand, on the gnarly, pointy bit on the apex of the wax shell. The very thought of this sent her weak at the knees, all funny peculiar and fearful of falling over.

Then the container had to be cupped in both hands and gently squeezed, releasing the tasty, finely-ground meat preparation in a nectar spurt. This caused my wife to gasp and utter more profound, negative beseechments towards me that I desist in my attempt to avail myself of lapping mince from this, this wonderfully, original, male-inspired sachet.

Therefore, I cannot yet pronounce a verdict on whether Al Felloverian mince is superior to our own, though it does sound a tasty recipe.

However, the receptacles should find rising favour amongst our male members. I will forward a motion at our next meeting that we, as the premier Mince Front in Annan, adopt immediately the Al Felloverian method of taking mince.

The Al Felloverian Mince Front donated several loaded Mince mamaries to our cause. They will be available for handling and sampling by members at our next meeting. I have told members it's first come, first served, to pucker their lips and not to tell their missus's.

Annan Mince Front Parable To Holyland Pilgrims

The official Nazareth and Judea Kosher Mince Front officials insisted, on the arrival of the invited, installed members of The Annan Mince Front, at Nazareth International Airport, that the N.M.J.K.F should not to be confused in any way with the Tuareg imposters; namely, members of the Unclean Mince Front for Nazarea and Judeth.

In their Minceoleum, their Great Hall of mince mysticism, we saw N.J.M.K.F installed officials preparing for their annual portrayal of 'The Biblical Christmas Parable: 'Extravaganza of the One-thousand-and-Fifty Doughboys and the Four-hundred Kilos of kibbutz reared buffalo mince'. This more realistic metaphor replaces the fable of the five loaves and two fishes feeding the 5000 souls, hatched on Galilee's banks by religious people who, in the time of Jesus, thought they'd wolfed much more than they had.

Nazareth, the place where Jesus spent his childhood and youth, is located in the lower Galilee, in the heart of a valley, surrounded by mountains that embrace several of the most important mince manufacturing kibbutzim of today's and yesteryear's Holy Land.

Mince manufacture began in the Galilee region about 3,000 years ago; Nazarene mince becoming known as the best, or steak mince as we'd call it today, low in fat and gristle and a staple in the diet of Byzantines. News of the delicious Nazarene Mince spread along the Mediterranean, then it turned north. Records show 'mince and tatties' as a staple of the Scots, some years before the battle where English hordes attempted to burn the bannock, near a burn, somewhere nearby the treacly wee town of Bannock.

Close to the White Mosque in Nazareth, a place where men wearing funny, muslin habits go to bow and pray many times, each time the Mincesupremo, a man skilled in Arabic twitter, calls them to prayer from high in his minceret, stood the original mincing kibbutzim of Kfar Nakhum and Sde Boker.

Without effective Health and Safety legislation, these now defunct grinding houses of kibbutz-reared buffalo meat had turned somewhat unhygienic, smelly and disgusting. Nevertheless, for one-hundred years they had attracted mince travellers from all continents to their wayside kiosks. Sitting on those stubbly verges, these pilgrims scoffed the mince as the disciples had scoffed it, with doughboys, slow and delicately risen; they experienced all the smells, flavours and, unfortunately, the intestinal parasites associated with an authentic, Middle Eastern feeding frenzy.

Such pilgrimages ended in the first century AD, but in recent times, due to the invention of anti-diarrheal drugs like Imodium, mince pilgrims are returning to the region. A major attraction is the Museum of Israeli Mince Production, BC/AD, located in Nazareth's underground passages.

However, during the recent rocket attacks, Israeli chemists sold out of Imodium. From our own experiences, we suggest that, before flying out, today's Pilgrims wishing to research Nazarene mince, should stock up with the quick-acting version of the drug and the anti-parasitic, tapeworm mangler, Metronidazole.

The Annan Mince Front Budget Influence

Annually, the Chancellor of the Exchequer invites dignitaries of the United Kingdom's regional Mince Fronts to visit him in his bean-counting house at 11 Downing Street. Last Wednesday, a week before today's budget, the Chancellor welcomed the A.M.F party from Annan.

George asked me, as Grand Wizard of the Ancient Collop, what he could do to boost mince consumption and the economy within the four countries. He hinted that his budget would contain many features pleasing to the electorate, but conceded that cheaper mince was high on his agenda and its provision the truest way to achieve a further five years in power for the Tories, without the policy hindering, rag-tag-and-bobtail, mince rejectionists that are their present coalition partners.

I advised that he should not increase petrol and diesel duties as many mince lovers needed transport to reach the butchers of their choice, and that he should scrap the beer-duty escalator, reduce the price of a pint, for beer was an appetiser that all mince aficionados appreciated, especially before sitting down to a plate of mince and tatties.

I also suggested that cheaper, more-easily purchasable housing was the key to overcrowding in homes where mince was the staple, and would definitely give the mince economy a boost.

As I listened to George's speech today, it was evident that he had taken on board many of my suggestions.

In reply to the budget, The Right Honourable Mr Ed. Maybebland, leader of the opposition and de facto supporter of the phoney, preposterous, discredited, disreputable mince front for Annan, made no mention whatsoever of the Labour party's mince agenda.

Annan Mince Front Receives A Call From The Vatican

The Annan Mince Front were, on Wednesday 13th, pleased to receive a call from Cardinal Tritare Di Manzo, the Vatican City's newly appointed head of mince procurement, immediately on the election of the Argentinean Cardinal Tagliatelli Googoglestye as Pope.

Cardinal Di Manzo requested the presence of me, Grand Wizard of the Ancient Collop, in the Vatican kitchens, the next day. The Argentine pope, raised in this mainly meat eating country, had revealed his penchant for beef mince and Scotch pies as staples in his diet.

In particular, Cardinal Di Manzo asked me to procure and take with me a dozen Francis' pies, from their bakery in High Street, Annan. Apparently, when quite young and as plain Father Googoglestye, he had toured Scotland and had attended a football match at Galabank; there, at halftime, in a game between Annan Athletic F.C. and Arbroath F.C., he partook of a pie which he enjoyed, its succulence he never forgot.

Was this memory instrumental in the choice of name he gave himself, we may ask? Was it down to a Scotch pie? Or, more likely, a minced-mutton pie baked in Annan: the Francis' pie?

I realised quickly this was a nailed on opportunity to advertise the A.M.F's dedication to mince dishes, mutton or beef, to a billion or so Catholics worldwide and the 2000 or so hearty and loyal Falkland islanders who, for generations, have persevered with minced mutton as their staple.

Annan Mince Front Members Are Guests To The S.M.P

The Annan Mince Front is, unquestionably, Scotland's premier mince protector and absolute believer in the dish's health-giving properties. Today, we were guests of the S.M.P., The Scottish Mince Party, at the Holyrood Parliament building.

The universe seeks our advice on all things mince. This invitation had to come from the S.M.P.

Although we think the Holyrood parliament an unnecessary tier of government and the building a 'white elephant', we were delighted to accept.

We also discovered that the S.M.P isn't a pro-mince party, the acronym a predictably horrible, party-leader-inspired bluff used to confuse gullible Scots. The A.M.F therefore takes issue with S.M.P's independence-from-mince agenda.

With a somewhat split personality of a surname, their leader, Mr. Salomon Stew-Art, in our opinion, has delusions of grandeur. The A.M.F have learned that he prays for supporters to erect a statue of him, opposite the castle in Princes Street, Edinburgh, before the polls deliver their verdict on mince dependency.

Mr. Salomon Stew-Art sees himself as Prince Salomon of the Antimincers, and those misguided Scots who want severance from all-things-mince recognise him as such a person. He will be popular amongst the miserly twenty-per-cent of Scottish mince rejectionists, if a sculptor chisels the statue from compressed Quorn, the long-life, counterfeit alternative to the 'real thing'.

Although the Stew-Art family has its roots firmly entrenched in the poorest area of Teuchterdom, they've never favoured mince as a staple. This boast is enshrined in their family crest: optimum bubulae pro nobis, quoniam massarum scindunt. Translated from Latin the meaning is, the best of beef for us; mince for the masses.

Most Union supporters will believe, as we do, that any of Salomon Stew-Art's statements on mince independence will contain phoney, misleading information. How could it not be when, historically, the family have shunned the nourishing dish?

For all his independence rhetoric, Mr. Salomon Stew-Art did not convince us that the art of making a pot of stew over the magic of a pan of mince would have the Scots voting, in their droves, to reject mince. Or other European countries would vote to keep us in the Europe Mince Union, The E.M.U.

Quite clearly, if becoming an independent country, the Maastricht Mince Mountain will not have the Scottish ladle dipping into it for a share. We believe that Scotland's split of the M.M.M will be small: not much more than the scrapings from a manicured Milngavie-lawn molehill, if a mole ever had the temerity to dig one into existence there.

The A.M.F opposes independence from the rest of mince loving United Kingdom.

Annan Mince Front Welcome A Belgian Delegation

The Annan Mince Front welcomed the Belgian delegation representing the Low Country's Ground Horsemeat Authority.

At our Mincing Wynd headquarters this week we entertained a dignified gent from Gent: Horace Nektar Del Dobbin, with the grand title, Opperste opzichter Grondpaardvlees Del Belgie, together with Gigi Del Dobbin, his charming wife, and their daughter, Ambrozijn Equines del Dobbin.

At the meeting attended by several Dumfriesshire mince aficionados, Horace outlined some of Belgium's relationship with horsemeat.

Belgium, which is one of the few remaining horse-eating countries in the world, together with the Netherlands, Germany, Switzerland, Austria, Sweden, Italy and France, as well as Asian and South American countries, consume horse at the rate of 50 million a year. *A lot of also-rans end up her, methinks?*

In Flanders, the eating of *paard,* or horse, traces its roots to hard labour. A few hundred years ago, the town of Lokeren, East Flanders, used to be a small port city, which required the presence of many horses to haul and transport cargo. Famous for their strength, the Brabant horses would work until knackered before slaughter for mince.

A nicer alternative is having horse in a *belegde broodje.* Smoked horsemeat sold in many sandwich shops tastes very similar to bresaola, the Italian air-dried beef. Dark reddish brown in thin slices, the most significant taste is that of the smoke itself. Meert's butcher shop not only smokes its own sandwich meat, it makes its own horse salami.

Also known as Boulogne-sausage, after a French port city that also utilised horses like Lokeren did, Belgian horse salami is easy to recognise for its traditional square shape. Shoppers can find both smoked horse and salami in butchers and grocery shops. Just look for the Dutch word *paard.*

Today, the E.U. registers Lokeren horse sausages for having historical and culinary significance. Based on the same traditional recipe, the horsemeat is no longer from exhausted workhorses but comes from South America.

Annan Mince Front's Thoughts On Pretenders

A.M.F, Annan Mince Front has received a leaked memo from the files of the pretenders, the mince front for Annan.

In response to A.M.F's visit of the gents from esteemed Belgian city of Gent's ground horsemeat delegation, the mfa imposters have had visitors from the Iberian Peninsula 'eat-anything-with-a-hoof' brigade.

The horribly titled Carne capataz de caballo de la gula, Señor Willy de la Caballo no es el Burro, led the Iberian delegation. His son, Pene Del Burro, pero aún no Del Caballo, accompanied him.

On the Iberian's agenda was the conversion of British tastes to horsemeat mince: carne de caballo picada.

Our understanding of the situation in Spain and advice: Spanish horse ranches breed 100 thousand horses annually for human consumption. Because of the lengthy depression and rampant unemployment, Spaniards can no longer afford the luxury of sliced-meat-on-the-plate. They wish to export that superior meat to the UK and the rest of the E.U. Retained for their own consumption will be the rag end of caballo, burro joints and testicles, tongue, lights and tail. Minced, it will form the everyday picada seen on plates in Spanish homes.

Holidaymakers on the Costas should beware. The naturally-round meatballs in the delicious tomato and garlic sauces under the tapas counter in the many Spanish bars touting for trade might not be what they seem! Testículos en el ajo y la salsa de tomate they might just be!

Annan Mince Front Recipe Special

The public often ask the Annan Mince Front, the A.M.F, for special occasion recipes. Recently, a wife asked how she could ensure her husband came home from the pub early, especially on a Friday night, when they held what she called a 'Grab A Granny' night dance, at which he had tended to linger.

We assured her that, as her husband had a liking for mince, this recipe would do the job she had in mind, the garlic on her husband's breath guaranteeing the early return home. The remaining quantities, when frozen into portions, giving the same result each Friday for a month.

3 tbsp vegetable oil

3 onions, peeled, chopped

6 garlic bulbs, peeled and crushed

1 tsp chopped fresh thyme

1 tsp chopped fresh rosemary

1 kg/2¼lb beef mince

1 x 400g/14oz can chopped tomatoes

1 tbsp Worcestershire sauce

3 beef stock cubes

Preparation method

Heat half of the vegetable oil in a large pan over a high heat. Add the onions, all the garlic and herbs and fry for 3-4 minutes, or until softened and golden-brown. Turn off the heat and set the pan aside.

Heat half a tablespoon of the remaining oil in a separate pan over a medium heat. Add a third of the beef mince and fry for 4-5 minutes, or until browned.

Transfer the browned mince to the pan containing the onions, garlic and herbs.

Repeat the process twice more with the remaining oil and the remaining batches of mince. This browning process is essential with this quantity of mince.

Return the pan containing the cooked mince and vegetables to a medium heat. Add the Worcestershire sauce and stir the mixture well to combine. Bring the mixture to a simmer.

Crumble the stock cubes into a large heatproof jug and add 1 litre/1¾ pints of boiling water. Stir until the stock cubes have dissolved.

Add the stock to the mince and bring to a simmer. Simmer for one hour, uncovered, or until the volume of liquid has reduced slightly and the sauce has thickened.

Diners can eat the braised mince immediately, served with mashed spuds, rice or spaghetti.

Annan Mince Front Advice To Our Australian Cousins

Annan Mince Front dignitaries were hopping mad this week on opening an Email from Mr. Joey Pouch, founder of Australia's Melbourne Mince Front. The message conveyed New Year greetings from the M.M.F to the A.M.F, but contained, as an attachment, the following, nonsensical request: 'Please can you send us any recipes you have for kangaroo mince?'

We didn't mince our words and boxed off this response: the kangaroo is a native Australian species, its meat edible and consumed in great quantities by Aborigines, immigrants, and, from the size of them, Aussie Rugby players and some of Australia's fattest men.

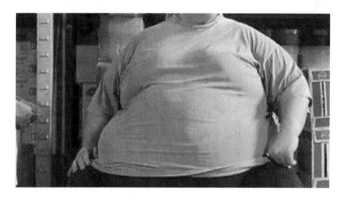

Kangaroo steaks, chops, roasts and bouncing wallaby bangers are barbie favourites, the bones and week-old road kill making flash 'marsoupials'.

There's 58.6 million of the species using the outback for moon-launch practice. They're not all as friendly or as intelligent as Skippy was, but are catchable by skilled hunters with boomerangs, a kind of curved sticks fitted with a homing device. We do not get a kick telling you this, but there'll be umpteen recipes lurking in the culinary treasure troves of Victorian ladies with a bent for cooking. Without doubt, the Ned Kelly gang will have salted away recipes, probably burying them in time capsules near the foot of Uluru, top-right corner, six feet to the north, marked with an X, for future use, to prepare a tasty, ground-meat variation to the satisfaction of the discerning, Aussie palate.

To prove the aforementioned, we also reminded Joey of the sacred words enshrined in the Aussie national anthem from time immemorial: 'Andy sang as he watched and waited for his mince to boil, under the shade of a billabong tree, who'll come scoffing kanga mince with me? Andy sang as............................ ?'

We hear rumours that these creatures exist in Britain, mainly in the wilder parts of the mainland: the peak district and Scotland's Highlands. Sightings suggest the roos appear scared, don't bounce away, but camouflage themselves behind high vegetation, to peer and discern if the approaching hiker were a gullible Australian tourist waving his mince recipe from home. The roos' actions are clear: we don't wish to become mince.

The A.M.F does not wish to upset all those decent Ausie folks who still believe in the legend Skippy.

The Annan Mince Front Attend Time-Capsule Exhumation

This week, the Dumfries & Maxwelltown Academy of Archaeologists called in at The Annan Mince Front headquarters in Mincing Lane, Annan. The archaeologists were seeking answers to the findings at their dig at the White Hart Hotel car park, Dumfries, Scotland. For our expertise in certain matters mince, they invited me, as Grand Wizard of the Ancient Collop, and other office bearers, along to the unveiling of ancient artefacts contained in the time capsule discovered there.

The White Hart Hotel, the popular live music venue, in Brewery Street, Dumfries, has had a history of entertaining Doonhamers and visiting inebriates with music, song and dance for more than 300 years. It might have entertained, on several occasions, The Bard himself, Rabbie Burns, who frequented renowned public houses, to carouse, spout his own poetry and song.

In its time, the White Hart has been a hostelry, staging Inn and, for hundreds of years, a live music venue of some repute. In its early days, with stables out the back and accommodation, it housed resident ostlers and offered hay-filled palliasses to comic singers and itinerant musicians with or without dancing bears.

On site, we saw the time capsule, buried there circa 1790. Contained in the capsule were a touring shroud and a death mask, which a travelling showband, with the wonderfully evocative title 'Mince', had donated to the interring of late, eighteenth century relics.

A Google search did reveal the existence of the popular showband 'Mince', active about that period. One account suggests that, straight from gigs on The Paps of Dura, and The Kyles of Bute, where they played at the festival 'Adoration of the Haggi', 'Mince' travelled over lonely, stony roads by donkey-pulled cart to Dumfries, to play the White Hart venue.

The Brewery Street Scrolls, flimsy paper documents, old, so rare and revealing of Doonhamer life of that period, which we, as curators of the Mince Museum, keep in a secret, environment-protective location, also mention the showband's existence and the sell-out gigs played at the White Hart.

Information becomes sketchy, but a careful peep at the Scrolls reveals that, at the start of the nineteenth century, the showband commenced a European tour, which was to end in Gaggastan, the showband vocalist's native country.

However, en-route there, in the small, Black Forest town of Zimmerstadt, they performed a warm-up gig that didn't go down well with the Zimmerstadtians. Thinking that giving the showband a Germanic name would make them more popular, they chose 'Panzermince'. The locals took exception to the demeaning of their language and chased them out of town quoting; German mince is and always has been organic and free of any corrupting ingredients. We at A.M.F aren't too sure about this!

'Mince' lead fiddle player, trianglist and tambourinist, Alexis Wilton 3rd, in 1799, wrote the words of what today we would call a Heavy Metal number. The song went something like this: Make me a tough old ploughshare, sharp and easily scything through loam, clay or rock-strewn ground, you hard working, Doonhamer blacksmith with thumbs like battered sausage rolls, in your smiddy, hot, smoky and sparky, on your anvil black with coal dust and well dented from missing with your mighty hammer.

Vocals: Gaggastanian refugee Bruno Silkivox.

On spoons and bones: Felix Sticks.

Double bass: Ivor Upright.

Tambourinist, triangle and regular fiddle: Alexis Wilton 3rd.

If anyone knows of a similar band, Dumfries is screaming out to hear it.

Annan Mince Front Thoughts On Poor Immitation

As Grand Wizard of the Ancient Collop of the Annan Mince Front, I learned that the phony, distrusted, pretenders to the mince throne, 'the mince front for Annan', have declared they are aware of a source of high quality cow/horse mince to which no mince-loving person or government agency could object. They propose the unbridled unleashing onto the meat markets of Britain and the rest of the World, of flesh from the fabulous hybrid the jumart (pictured).

Information for the unwary: the jumart is the fabled offspring of the mating between a bull and a mare or she ass, or vice versa. Journals dated circa 1755 described the jumart as small animal, excessively loud, with the head of bull, large of nose, but without horns, and broad shouldered.

In those days, the naturalist, Georges-Louis Leclerc, Comte de Buffon, a contemporary of Charles Darwin, expressed doubts that such a creature existed, but thought that if one ever had, then, because of its propensity to bellow loudly, it would be female.

The A.M.F can inform to you that the jumart is a mythical creature, whose presence only existed in ancient writings of the eighteenth century: fairy tales.

There is no proof of their existence then, or today. We also suspect such matings would be problematic. The cow being the intended mother it would experience the unexpected hungness of the stallion attempting penetration and would hirple rapidly away. The mare, the intended mother, she might not notice the minisculeness, by comparison, of the bull's penetration. Unwilling to carry the bull's weight, it's likely she would just saunter off in the direction of fresh pastures.

Quite clearly, 'the mince front for Annan' is flogging a dead jumart!

Greek Mince Authority Beseechment

This week, Drastic Skintosavaloi, president of The Greek Beef Mince Authority, approached the Annan Mince front, desperate to elicit assistance to alleviate another dire situation besetting his country. As Grand Wizard of the Ancient Collop, I was able to offer him help.

Drastic lamented: 'Beef stocks in my country are more depleted than the Euro supply in this stricken land. For the first time in two thousand and fifteen years, the Marathon pie-eating contest could be cancelled. There isn't enough mince in the entire country, or the readies to import any, to allow the ancient contest to proceed.'

Drastic whined: 'The two million workers normally employed in the once extensive but now depleted mousaka, papoulsakia and hillopites making industries, seasonally recruited to become pie makers, fear redundancy. Twenty million pensioners are reduced to begging for leftovers outside Kentucky Fried Olive joints. Neither Germany nor France has active Mince Fronts, and my requests to their Mince Beef Authority Premiers, no less, has received (*oxi*) *no* positive responses.

'Zeus, King of the Gods, would have thrown thunderbolts at the politicians now running Greece, would have taken up bow and arrows and gone hunting wild cows to spare our beloved country the ignominy of going cap in hand to uncaring, European partners.....for anything.'

As *the* world authority on mince procurement, we were quickly able to source and procure ample beef stocks for mince-poverty-stricken Greece, in a neighbouring country, where Greeks might have feared the response to such a request.

We knew there are few cuisines in the world that have more creative uses for ground beef than the Turkish have. Turks use ground beef to make countless varieties of meatballs, kofte, musakka and karniyank.

An Email to Attilla Popeseyescu, Grand Fakir and Resident Magician of the Istanbul Mince Front, the advisers to the Turkish

Mince Procurement Authority based in Ankara, received a timely, positive response.

Attilla said, when revealing the immediate availability of ten forty-nine-foot containers, holding refrigerated, butchered beef sides from Eastern Anatolian Red cattle, bred and reared on the higher, Mount Ararat plains, which Turkey would provide free to their broke neighbours. 'It is gristly and jaw-taxing for the Greeks.'

As I prepare this report, a convoy of ten Daf trucks, hauling the altitude-toughened beef, head for the frontier crossing of Ipsala, en route to the pie-making kitchens of Marathon.

We of the Annan Mince Front wish for a more positive relationship between these neighbouring, mince loving countries to blossom from this sincere, jaw-dropping act of friendship.

Annan Mince Front Under Investigation

Local constabulary CID recently raided my office. As Grand Wizard of the Ancient Collop of the Annan Mince Front, the A.M.F, I found this intrusion into my domain distasteful in the extreme.

The A.M.F are renowned overseers of beef mince quality, production and procurement worldwide; and beyond, if cosmologists discover aliens needy of our guidance in all matters mince.

Many plain clothed Plod searched my office to gather evidence confirming the veracity of allegations of sexual harassment, groping, touching, indecency and other sexual deviancies, made against some of the membership.

Police stripped my office of all brochures; quality beef mince samples, (which were never returned), membership list and computer equipment. The detective sergeant explained: they were seeking pornographic material secreted on the computer hard-drive, that the members and I had access, thus giving credibility to the allegations.

I totally trusted my fellow officers and all members and so it proved: Plod found not a whiff of proof. I was always confident of their probity; perhaps because we do not have any politicians, film stars or pop stars as members.

I never had any doubts that the allegations were bogus. It was also my belief that members of the mince front for Annan, the amf, made the accusations anonymously, to sidetrack reports of their sexual deviancies, their wallowing in lewdness, existing within their ranks.

The mfa imposters are extraordinarily jealous of our leading position in all matters mince. Our collaboration with a prestigious English university was getting right up their noses. Together with the university microbiologists, we were developing the 'metabolic fingerprint', a precise method of detection, which meat-quality inspectors will use to identify precisely any amounts of pork or other meat contaminants polluting beef mince, thus ensuring the wholesome quality of beef mince on the open market.

The A.M.F is at the forefront of food-fraud investigations, principally in the adulteration of beef mince. We are the proud guardians of beef mince quality, too busily involved in our task to have time for any abnormal practices or the sending of fruity text messages, to anyone.

The considerable distance between the A.M.F and the mfa, in all matters mince, is quite spacey, excuse the pun, and so it will remain.

2018 Russia Football World Cup Request

We at the Annan Mince Front were today surprised when a letter arrived addressed thus: Аннан расчистил передние офисы говядины. Translation from Russian: Annan shredded beef front offices.

Apparently, a Russian immigrant, working in the Post Office international sorting office in London, quickly translated the address and arranged the letter's redirection to our well known, Worldwide-renowned, Annan Mince Front headquarters.

The letter's contents: a pigeon English written request from Boris Kutznutzov, Grand Wizard of the Mince Front Duma for Novochok. He required our expertise in selecting and procuring quality, uncontaminated beef mince which, he suggested, was not available in Russia, to feed the Russian World Cup squad. Thus energised and weaponised, the squad would play to athletic and soccer skill standards that teams of the other World Cup competing nation could not attain.

We were immediately suspicious on reading the letter's content: the use of a schoolboy name choice was the first clue leading us to conclude this was a foolish wind up, hatched by the idiots managing our phoney competitors in the mince procurement and quality protection business, the mince front for annan.

On checking our office door handles, we found a substance, which looked like a dollop of what I have seen adhering to my car roof this summer, as seagulls swarm overhead. These winged, white rats are desperate for a meal, but are still full of excrement.

I think the unscrupulous bunch of mfa chancers had a better prospect of fooling us, had they used the City of Minsk as the source of their request.

Presence Requested At All Exits

The request from the England football team manager, Roy (not of the Rovers) Fussy-Headjob, to yours truly, Grand Wizard of the Ancient Collop of the Annan Mince Front, the A.M.F, was a complete surprise to the membership and me. "Please fly immediately to Nice and prepare a humiliation, complète et totale" minuit fête de hachee de beouf a la Francaise, for my vanquished team, following their match with Iceland".

That the request arrived the day before the match was even more shocking.

It was if Roy (maybe of Jiangsu Rovers quite soon) had expected his squad to mince their way to defeat in the match, the most important since the last World Cup.

It struck several of my members that the request indicated Roy's lack of confidence in his team and was predicting their defeat in the Stade de Nice, at the hands, or as it turned out, to the cool, skilled, ball-controlling feet and long-throw techniques of the Icelanders. This prompted a steady stream of my more astute, form-reading members to visit Ladbrokes and there to wager considerable pounds of their hard-earned cash, at good odds, on an Iceland victory. After the result, Annan Mince Front members rejoiced in Annan hostelries. The mincing of the England players was, indeed, head and shoulders above that of the blonde, clean-headed-and-dandruff-free-shoulders of the Icelanders.

I was unable to accede to Roy's request. I had previously accepted an invitation to prepare, in the kitchen of a London redoubt, the temporary fortification of some well-known Brexiteers, a victory meal of high quality beef mince, heavy with garlic and liberal with red wine jus, served on a platter of mash. I thought it a nice touch to prepare my menu thus: boeuf haché de qualité, lourd avec de l'ail et vin rouge jus liberal et purée pommes de terre.

However, my menu idea deflated like a lead balloon, as was mentioning *the war* to the French. Brexiteers were attempting to avoid any discontent with continental Europe.

It was plain, yet quality British fare of mince and mashed tatties that the victorious LEAVE campaigners tucked into.

Mincexit

As Grand Wizard of the Ancient Collop of the Annan Mince Front, the A.M.F, I oversee mince preparation, fat reduction techniques, organic-additive selection and sourcing novelty-value catering accessories, worldwide and beyond. During the ongoing Brexit negotiations taking place in Brussels, I am representing my membership and the concerns of British people, to ensure a good deal for mince. I have intimated to the main negotiators that, when the Common Mince Policy ceases to exist, we would want the free movement of mince across borders to remain in place. "Mince without borders" is our goal and we will persist in our efforts to ensure a successful outcome on March 2019.

Representatives from many of Europe's Mince Fronts and Beef Mince Authorities joined me in these discussions. Drastic Skintosavaloi, president of The Greek Beef Mince Authority, expressed his appreciation of our past efforts to alleviate a beef mince shortage in his country. Attilla Popeseyescu, Grand Fakir and Resident Magician of the Istanbul Mince Front, stated he was pleased to have aided the Greeks! Horace Nektar Del Dobbin, with the grand title, Opperste opzichter Grondpaardvlees Del Belgie, together with Gigi Del Dobbin, his charming wife, and their lovely daughter, Ambrozijn Equines del Dobbin, were supportive of our cause. Cardinal Tritare Di Manzo, the Vatican City's latest head of mince procurement, delivered the Pope's blessing on our negotiations. The official Nazareth and Judea Kosher Mince Front, although not involved in any negotiations, were eager listeners to our debates.

Mr. Joey Pouch, founder of Australia's premier, Melbourne Mince Front, sat in, made no suggestions on our policy, but offered his support if we required a World Free Trade deal and safe shipping of mince from the Antipodes.

The Scottish Mince Party, the despised S.M.P, refused to attend, their case for remincing aligned with the imposters of the mfa, the mince front for Annan

Mince In The News

USA media report that the inability of American housewives to cook mince to their spouses' satisfaction is the greatest challenge to a lengthy marriage and the single-most factor in marriage breakdown. The Mincinnati State University survey also found that males survive splitting up better if they had watched their mothers cook mince to their father's satisfaction, and can turn their hands to this skill following divorce. Mincinnati State, for the first time since its inauguration, will offer mince cookery with tearless onions, to women, up to degree standard, in an effort redress this national problem.

Money Talks

Recent newspaper headlines have alerted readers to the resignation of Rab Prancey, head of The Mincery Bank. Prancey's downfall was his embroilment in the Limincebor interest-rate fiddle, where he instructed his bank to charge zero rates of interest to rogue mince-importer borrowings. In an interview, an implausible excuse tripped from the lips of the guilty head banker: we were turning our nation into a global super power. The importation of EU mince, willy nilly, at lower cost, will feed our peoples cheaply and empower them to work harder in their employments for the benefits of all.

In our opinion, Rab is kidding. We know that industry and The City cannot produce wealth without mince greasing the wheels of commerce. However, Scots know that the jaw-slackening, tough beef of continental Europe production systems is an abomination, not the same as granny churned out to feed our nation in times of need and the government should banish it from our dinner tables. We will not fall for perpetrations of these dodgy mince dealers in the now disreputable City.

Archaeological Discovery Adjacent

The Proposed Whitesands Flood Defences In Dumfries

The significant archaeological discovery made during the removal of important, buried Whitesands' and Brewery Street artefacts, before the laying of foundations for the proposed Nith flood defences, went unmentioned by local media. Excavations twenty feet to the north of the old staging inn, The White Hart Hotel, on the spot where, 461 years ago, stage coaches left for such wonderfully named places like Ae, Palnacky and faraway Dunragit, unearthed a 1-litre time capsule, buried there then by Dumfries musical fanatics.

Eye-opening, time capsule revelations suggest that a Bavarian-based touring band, similar in style to the wonderful Dumfries band Goggsies Midnight Scunners, and highlighted as the "band to be watched" by Nostrdamus in one of his few revealing prophecies containing an element of truth, played Dumfries venues in those times.

Excitingly named for that era, "Googleyes Mitternacht Panzermince" was a ten-piece progressive-oompah band that flirted with Germanic martial music, rocking it up on stage.

Suitably attired in skin-tight lederhosen, touring shrouds and BIG HAIR adorned with seagull feathers, found in profusion near the river Nith, they played their short and long-necked lutes and bongos. Strutting like peacocks, with arrogance and pomposity, the Kavalier bandsmen sought to own the stage, whilst receiving great applause and approval from those old-time, Doonhamer headbangers.

Female Groupies, reputedly large-of-fist and capable of carrying by the handles six frothy steins in each hand without spillage, conscripted from a tribe of giants residing deep in the Black Forest, provided refreshments from huge, imported barrels of Bavarian I.P.A to local imbibers.

159

The presence of these mighty, soon-to-be-emptied *bierfässer*, (beer barrels) assured the Bavarian band's boozy tradition living on in memory. Present-day Goggsies Midnight Scunners band-members keep those distant memories alive, in all of their gigs.

Tunnel Symphony:

There's been much twittering on local online sites-of-interest regarding ancient tunnels connecting Dumfries town's various historic buildings, still standing, crumbled with age or demolished. The council aren't about to lash money at the locating of and opening of the tunnels to the public in a safe condition for exploration.

Twenty-five years ago, the then owners of the White Hart Hotel in Brewery Street discovered the entrance to an ancient tunnel in their car park. The hotel owners entered the tunnel, discovering it was a natural channel, hewn from the substrata by persistent rain and Nith flooding, and that it ran uphill, parallel with Friars Vennel, to peter out beneath Barclay's Bank.

Musicians playing the White Hart venue found the tunnel had remarkable echo-chamber qualities and were keen to use the facility to make superb recordings. Dragging P.A equipment down the tunnel entrance proved impossible. However, that wonderful Dumfries band Goggsies Midnight Scunners played an acoustic set down there. Goggsie was in good voice, while band members contributed their musical brilliance.

Safety concerns caused the closure of the tunnel; however, even today, if you were to put your ear close to the false drain located behind the hotel, the only entrance now on view, you will hear the musician's harmonious beat and Goggsies' dulcet tones reverberating along the disused passage. The natural timbre of this echo chamber is enhancing the remnant vibrations of the acoustic set that experts say will endure for all time.

Music aficionados can find the answer to this phenomenon in one of hundreds of laws of acoustics; namely, a complex mix of geometry, architecture, physics and neuro science, that nature has mastered to make Goggsies music still sound so beautiful.

Music lovers today must possess caving expertise to experience this phenomenon today or catch them at a gig.

Mince In The News

Mince thickly plasters today's newspapers. One cheeky commentator impudently claims that he once took mince with the Queen Mum at Balmoral. Cherie Blair is spending this weekend at the Queen's Deeside estate with husband, Tony. In preparation of her visit, the butchering of twenty Aberdeen Angus cattle took place in the royal abattoir. Local mincers, bearing the royal seal of approval, then rendered the beasts into mince-size chunks to satisfy the demands of Cherie's mince-scoop-shaped gob.

The mince-snubbing upper classes have also had coverage. It seems these classes were responsible for turning our nation into a global economic superpower. Come on, you're kidding me. Everyone knows that without mince… nothing works.

Emigration has reporters leaping over each other in an effort to convey the most devastating of scenarios. The most serious of these reports suggests the imminence of a bottomless mince drain, as our national dish becomes the staple of 100million immigrants.

Such is the power of mince that the Poles are using 'reverse mincing' to tempt their British-based citizens into returning home. Hearing of these blown-away citizens' addiction to our national staple, the Polish government have offered two kilos of steak mince per family member, per week, free of charge. What a carrot! That's the power of mince when combined with carrots, and the Polish authorities know this.

A Harley Street doctor this week admitted that mince was the main ingredient in his elixir of eternal youth. Mince injections were, apparently, a far too costly method of firing the secret ingredient into aging, wrinkly-skinned bodies to bring about the youthful affect. Badgered by reporters, he revealed his secret method of mince ingestion. Take 1kilo of mince, 3 large onions, 3 carrots, ½ teaspoon each of salt and pepper and 1 beef stock cube, simmer all ingredients in a pan over a small flame until tender, then serve on a plate with buttered potatoes and cabbage.

Some of the public say that Maggie Becket's the most powerful woman in Britain. Sorry. Ask any British housewife who's withheld mince from her hubby's weekly menu because she's not getting her oats regularly, and you'll have the definitive answer from her. Moi!

Mince In The News

Mince in the headlines again. Himalayan Super Mince, said to slow aging and increase the sex drive, officially goes on sale 'over the counter', in Britain, for the first time today.

Mince addicts will know that this product has been available for many years, 'under the counter' of many disreputable mince-hawker's kiosks and backstreet mince emporiums. A natural Viagra, H.S.M works its wonders in the twinkling of a nymphomaniac's eye. These incorrigible females recognise quickly the benefits of a product containing ten times more iron than normal mince.

Scientists have also discovered that without mince, men's Body Mass Index goes to pot, their infertility factor wallows, and they can easily gain 10 kilos of weight during a mince free supper.

Interesting news coming out of The Punjab tonight suggests The Scots first introduced mince to The Indian subcontinent. Previous thinking put the Dutch up for the accolade, by purchasing Goa in 1823 from the resident, drug-fuelled Goanese, by offering a chalice of a tasty stew, consisting space cake and ground water buffalo meat. Now, it seems, the Dutch are only to blame for introducing the meatball, which became the kofta. A photograph exists of a water buffalo resting before receiving a brain hammering and a sharp knife to the jugular in the lobby of an Indian mince-processing facility. Apparently, a blown-away Jock called MacDonald flattened out these meaty spheres, making them fit into a bun. It's still all mince at the end of the day: no big deal.

Mince In The News.

Mince causes Polish taxi driver some confusion. Two Southampton girls wanted him to take them to Mince, a small, but on the map, Hampshire hamlet. Entering Quorn into his sat-nav system, he ended up taking them to Leicestershire, the home of the Quorn Hunt.

Nine Glasgow firefighters have complained of being forced to attend diversity training, for refusing to hand out mince during a gay pride rally. Surely, distributing mince on such an occasion is part of their work agreement. Mincing requires mince and without it, there would be no such parade, and nothing to keep them in a job.

Only one-in-four of Scotland's population think mince is of better quality under Alec Salmond. Rising fat and gristle levels in this staple, since S.N.P came to power, has three Scots in four wishing for the return of Maggie Thatcher, Mince Snatcher.

Cherie Blair and Partners were involved in more top-level court cases involving mince than any other barristers' chambers it emerged yesterday. Their successes marked another boom year for Mince, ensuring adherence to quality control under the new Mince Rights Act 2008.

Mince In The News.

Jittery Star Trek legend Willie Shatner has refused a plate of mince, complete with doughboys floating in the rich meaty sauce. He says he's willing to march into the unknown, seek out new life and civilisations, but he must know the planets are mince-free before he'll set foot there. This goes to prove that the Americans won't go boldly when it comes to trying the more succulent items on a space menu.

Mince-free districts of Glasgow have the highest death rate in the city, health authorities today commented. Inhabitants living in these areas have a lifespan of forty years less than where mince is a staple. A Glasgow M.S.P has accused the Scottish Executive of not educating Scots on the health benefits found in eating mince. He insists he'll show the way forward and have gourmet mince served in the Holyrood canteen next session; he'll also vote for a cheaper variety to be included on school dinner menus, and mince sciences added to curriculums!

A lonely heilandman of teuchter stock has put a notice in a shop window in his hometown. He's looking for feminine, fun-loving mince lovers to make contact with him. He hopes his other stipulations will weed out any not-so-devoted-would-be mince partners: they must be nutty, but not talk or nag a lot and not be too big or hefty. He's already had a couple of long calls from daft, drooling wimmen who haven't looked in the mirror recently!

Mince Here And There.

The threat of mince shortages in The Canaries, caused by the million African illegal immigrants arriving daily on the islands, is worrying the Madrid Government.

The suspension of bull fighting until the shortage ends is under serious consideration, states the Spanish Prime Minister. An unsympathetic Brussels has laid the blame squarely at the doors of the Spanish Congress of Deputies, citing the Spanish mince amnesty of 2005 for the existing famine conditions.

The E.E.C Burgermeat Minister said: the Mince Mountains will remain closed to these illegals, and that they could go back to their African homelands and scoff on fillets of monkey there.

The inability of wives to cook mince to a husband's satisfaction is the biggest single factor in marriage breakdown, according to Ohio State University, USA. Men, however, survive the split better because they watched their mothers cook mince to their father's satisfaction, and can turn their hand to this skill after the divorce. Now, the university is offering 'mince cookery with tearless onions' courses for women, up to degree standard, in an effort to redress this national problem.

Only in uneducated parts of the world do householders still bait mousetraps with lumps of cheese. From Burn's poem 'Ode to a Mouse', they should have learned that Scotland also wasn't rodent free and that we had the answer.

Cheese, that universal rodent temptation, was rarely successful at enticing a wee Jock moose to lay its head down on the block. But we Scots got clever: along came mince, the real bait, the real deal, the 'wee moose's' favourite. And since Jock Trapp invented the attachment that successfully held the 'wee baw o' mince' in place on his spring-loaded device… as a nation we've been 'moose' free.

LIAR OF THE YEAR

Robbie Beaghan won the All Ireland Liar of the Year Contest for 57 years on-the-belt-end. Held in the Navigator's Den public house, in the small town of Ballyfallacy, he'd thrashed all purveyors of untruths. In those years, no contestant outlied him. Although renowned and feted as the best liar that the island of Ireland had ever produced, he knew fibbers with potential, lurking in the wings, were dreaming up fictions, honing their fables, waiting for him to falter. He always had to have a better fib to impress the wise men judging the competition and this year again, he was sure he had the best lie ever told.

Both Robbie and his wife Molly were 78 years old. Molly had remonstrated to Robbie since his last conquest that it was time to quit the competition. 57 years of winning the same prize, a fortnight holidaying in a horse-drawn, gypsy caravan in County Donegal, had become both tedious and painful. Her ageing backside had suffered the buffeting of potholed, country tracks in the unsprung vehicles. The jig jogging mulish, surly brutes between the shafts, masquerading as horses, never seemed to miss a rut or boulder and she didn't wish to suffer it all again.

The couple had circumnavigated the peaty waters of Lough Veagh 57 times, plodded through the forty shades of greenery of the Veagh national park, there and back, 114 times. Molly had watched Robbie gaze in awe for hours at flat topped Muckish mountain, 57 times, whilst bottoming a bottle of Old Paddy Whiskey. A part of the prize, the whiskey had done nothing to assuage the pain in Molly's backside or for her to show any love for equines. The very word assuage, in her mind, meant she was blameworthy for the old flab hanging from her backside.

For his 58th and consecutive entry into the competition, Robbie had a blockbuster of a lie to tell. He'd told Molly often enough during the months preceding the competition that he would be unbeatable once more, for sure. Not privy to Robbie's thinking, but sure that he'd never dare fib to her, Molly visited the contest pub to view the notice board there. Rumours abounded that, this year, alternative prizes were available for the victor to choose. And there it was, a prize that she'd be contented with: a Divan Suite. She'd insist he accept that prize instead of choosing to undertake another arduous, pony assisted, painful excursion around County Donegal. Lie to her, would he?

The highlight of the 11th of July that year, as it had been since 1906, in that part of the Island of Ireland, was The Liar of the Year Contest. Liar fans had been arriving at the venue since opening time. Several were becoming inebriated, singing morbid songs un-melodiously by the time the competition got underway. Most attendees were Robbie fans who were rigidly ignoring the fabrications of early contestants. Robbie's fans stood out by an Irish mile. All were dressed in the bib and tucker of the Irish labourer: the donkey jacket. Some had smartened up the attire with a black, string tie hanging from the collar of a white, nylon shirt.

The concert hall filled as Robbie's time approached. When the stage and hall lighting dimmed, and the spotlight above the competitor's entrance blazed into life, all knew his appearance was nigh. Onto the stage, an assistant carried the 'Lying Down Pouffe'. Stuffed with duck feathers and down, this leather-bound bag was there only for the previous year's winner of the competition to park his backside on, and so it had been since 1906.

Robbie, with a twinkle in both eyes, slid through the competitor's entrance sideways to rapturous applause and danced an impromptu jig as he took to the steps leading to the stage. When the curtains opened and the stage lights went up, Robbie was sitting cross-legged, recumbent on the pouffe.

When the shouts of 'Make it a good one Robbie,' and the hand clapping died, Robbie raised both arms for complete quiet, then he began his lie in his eloquent, Cork accent.

'Before the advent of the spade, but when the shovel was still the favoured tool of skilled navvies, the itinerant, tin pot teapot repairman and provider of illegal herbs, known as Shifty, made an earth-shattering discovery. Shifty lived in that hard to pinpoint mobile hamlet, with the ever-changing post-code, Randomtown. He was sitting up front of the leading caravan of the train, heading again for that night's stop at Randomtown. The night parking always had to offer a clean water supply and a wide tree to provide screened toilet facilities at the back of; all the trees at the stops, tall and broad of trunk, had growth nutrients provided in abundance over the years.

Alongside him sat his thick-hipped wife, Rosehip. Rosehip's maiden name was O'Hipps and Shifty had rescued her from a travelling circus that displayed her great arse as a national treasure.

'Shifty was puffing away merrily at his long-stemmed clay pipe, the smoke keeping at bay clegs and midges. He was gazing over the swishing tail and bobbing head of his pony when he saw a sneeze approaching along a track leading from a small wooded area. He would have seen it much earlier had he been looking towards the copse. He never liked the way he'd heard the word pronounced, thought it had portent for all dodgy dealers, never used the word himself in case it provoked a visit from the Garda. In shock, his teeth clamped down on the pipe stem, shattering it. He spat the pieces out and shouted loudly, "Heavens to O'Bloody Murgatroyd, I've just spotted something very interesting and I don't think it a parablepsis!"'

"A para what? What in the name o' the big man is one o' those?" Rosehip screeched deafeningly into Shifty's nearest ear.

'Tis mysterious, for sure, but I believe my eyes. As soon as I saw the sneeze, it disappeared. One of the little people was there on the same spot. Knee high to a grasshopper, he was, to be sure and wearing a wee suit. Then the sneeze was back again, for a split second, ephemeral like, about as long as a rat's fart would hang about in a wind tunnel. Then the wee fellah reappeared on the same spot. The wee fellah's gone again now and so is the sneeze. Begorrah an' Bejasus, that imp or leprechaun, whatever it was, but I'm sure it wasn't a banshee for there wasn't any wailing I could hear, must have gone through some bodily turmoil to pull off that trick, to be sure. Must have been a fierce sternutation. A sneeze of brobdingnagian proportions. A massive constuperation of his thropple to have caused that!'

"You're talkin' baloney again, to be sure you are, if you expect me to believe a tale the likes o' that. Brobdingnagian, you say. What kind of word is that? Never heard the likes," Rosehip responded, nodding her head sagely.

'Tis a big word from Gulliver's Travels that you wouldn't know about, to be sure,' Shifty answered.

'In his role as mobile herbalist, Shifty had listened to his customers tell of the magical concoction that only the little people possessed. Rumour had it that, when taken as a snuff, it enabled the little people to disappear in a sneezing fit when any danger loomed.

'Shifty had nothing as potent in his pharmacy, but he could see advantages in the ability to disappear. There was a market for such a substance. Many members of the caravan train disappeared under cover of darkness on a wild night, to return with eggs and chickens stolen from farmers' coops. He could change that into a daytime dodge for them. Rogues, who wished, together with any stolen loot carried, to vanish before the law could put a hand on a shoulder, would be his best customers.

'Shifty needed to source or discover the recipe for this explosive snuff. He needed to capture one of the little people, but had no idea how. For months, he kept his ear to the ground listening for another sneezing fit that would produce on the other side of the fierce sternutation a trappable imp.

'It was as the sun was quarter up that day when Shifty heard it. He was laid awake in the quiet of the Randomtown morning, alongside Rosehip, who had ceased her morning, heroic-snoring display that had rabbits crapping themselves, scurrying for their warrens. The staccato, reverberating sound must have come from elsewhere. He clambered out of the caravan onto the driving seat and listened intently. And there it was again, a sound like none he'd ever heard before: a sneeze, a cough, then a sneeze again then a strangulated cough and a sneeze rolled into one. Surely this was an imp of some sort and one who sounded distressed, wasn't in the best of health; an imp that he could trap much easier than a healthy, disappearing-in-a-flash one. Tracing the sound as coming from the steep hill to the east, Shifty quickly dressed and made his way towards the slopes, homing in on the sound.

'He rounded a bend in the track and there it was. No bigger than a tall standing grasshopper was the wee fella. Shifty could see the imp and the imp could see Shifty. The imp began to shake, seemingly trying to conjure up a sneezing fit, which would cause his disappearance. Shifty started to run towards the imp, reaching it whilst stooping low. With an outstretched hand, he grabbed it, before any vanishing act could take place.

'His hand tight around the wriggling creature, Shifty stuffed it into a fob pocket, which immediately began to leap about, a bit like a madly palpitating ticker. In a final, sudden mad lunge of desperation, the imp leapt at the fob lining, then all activity ceased.

'Shifty raced back to the caravan. Inside, he shook Rosehip to wakefulness, which was never an easy task. "I've captured an Imp," he cried out in delight and started to fumble with finger and thumb into the fob.

"What twaddle are you quoting to me now, you dolt," Rosehip responded loudly.

'Shifty lifted out of the fob several pieces of a miniscule man.

"To be sure and Bejasus it looks like pieces of a rattly old Hillman Imp, to me," Rosehip roared her assessment of the discovery.

'Groping deep in the fob, Shifty produced what he'd hoped to find: it was a tiny pouch, a scrotum sac that had been skilfully sliced from a toad. He hoped, in the tiny receptacle, he would find the miraculous snuff.

First, he had to test any contents. He looked at Rosehip. Yes, she would be the ideal guinea pig and if anything untoward happened to her, he would gain the space on the driving seat that her great arse occupied and have no loud, annoying cackle in his ears. A tincture or two remained in the pouch. Taking a pinch and laying it in a line on the back of his hand, Shifty offered it up to Rosehip's nose, and said, "Here, take a goodly sniff at this."

More compliant than usual, Rosehip consented and took a long inhalation, vacuuming the pinch into the upper reaches of her nasal cavity. The reaction of her body to the snuff was mind blowing. In the midst of an onrush of a humungous sneeze that would never reach fruition, the top of Rosehip's head shot off, spinning horizontally, creating a hole in the roof of the caravan as neat as any skilled cabinetmaker could carve with a fret saw.

'Today, all caravans have this addition. Travellers fitting the stack of a stove through the handy gap have smoke free, indoor cooking facilities and central heating.

'Supporters, whether you believe me or not, that is the last lie you'll hear me tell.'

Robbie admirers, who had stood in rapt silence, in respect, and to hear perfectly his words, missing nothing of the lie, erupted in cheering. The judges, fearing a dousing in the nearby stream had they voted otherwise, raised Robbie's arms high as the victor of the contest. All agreed: his lie was the best by an Irish mile.

Molly was standing on the home doorstep and in earshot of the adulation that she expected to erupt inside the pub. She smiled and turned as the roar hit her hearing, then scurried quickly though the house to the back yard. There, in a pile, stood the old family seating that she expected Robbie's prize to replace. Liberally sprinkled with paraffin, the pile burst into flame as the match made contact.

An hour later, Robbie and a posse of inebriated supporters assisted him in the cartage of the diving suit that Molly so desired. Today, viewers can see the suit standing, filled with cement and stiffly erect, in the corner of Robbie's garden.

The note hanging around its neck states: This is my tribute to all women who think they know best!

Signed,

Robbie Beaghan.

Monologues

Table of Contents

MONOLOGUE: THE ABSENT HUSBAND

The Husband:

My dad went to sea to earn a living. Some of his trips were two years long, the loneliness sending my mother a bit crackers. Just kidology, it turned out, to get him ashore. Times change and I reckoned I was dead lucky that the wife could accompany me on the ship after we were married. Jim boy didn't fancy the aggro dad suffered and still doesn't.

Morag had the time of her life whilst cruising across sun-drenched oceans, standing at the ship's rail at midnight looking into the infinite night. Visiting all those faraway places with strange sounding names was a thrill for her, too. Forever and a day she thought she'd be with me. Then she forgets to take her pill and gets a bun in the oven. I know I'm half to blame, but it was Hogmanay and I was drunk, too.

Don't get me wrong, I'm not averse to doing my bit in producing a family, but looking after them, that's the wife's job. I'm like my Dad; my job is making a decent wage, happily. And what I mean by that is: making a wage doing what I want to do, not what she wants me to do. And that's where the trouble lies; she wants me home, seeing me every night, working in a boring nine-to-five job for pennies. That's for Nancies, not for Jim boy. I value my freedom and I'm going to hang on to it as long as I can. My Dad was unhappy until the day he died because he had to leave the sea.

Imagine this. If you can't, I can. If Morag is anything like my mother, ships in San Francisco Bay will be able to hear the arguments we have in Govan, when Jim boy wants to go down to the pub for a game of pool with his pals.

It's bad enough now with the new satellite technology… I can hear the moans while I'm away. She can phone right into the ship, Skype me, wherever we are… loves that, she does. It's private, but she has the Captain's email address too, and through him, she sends me daft emails. The questions she asked are pathetic. 'When will you be coming home for good, dear?' she sends most of all. Shipmates wind Jim boy up, I can tell you. Granted, some seamen do creep off home leaving the good life behind at their wife's command... that's not for Jim boy, no way.

Her auld bag of a mother is no help. She pushes Morag to get me ashore, tells her she would never have stood it from her father. 'I had your Dad eating out of the palm of my hand when I was married and had a bairn on the way,' were words she used on Morag and have her change Jim boy.

Of course, the father in law's an old fart; works behind a counter in the family shop. The security and the fact that one day he'd own the business was probably the only attraction the mother in law saw in him. Now he's stricken, wouldn't say boo to a bloody goose... daren't. Henpecked and broken of mind that's how I'd sum him up... not a man at all, in my estimation...not a bit like Jim boy.

Morag's not going to turn me into a browbeaten, father-like figure. No one will intimidate Jim boy, like my mother bullied Dad, either. Next trip Jim boy will be signing on again; you wait and see.

The Mother in Law:

When I married John, the first thing I told him, on the way from the church to the reception, was: 'If you think you are going to treat me the way your father treated your poor mother, then you can think again. Seven bairns; worn out every day of her life she was running after them. And your father was squandering the shop takings down at the Rotary, boozing with his cronies. I will want you at home where I can keep an eye on you, John.'

He was not too happy about it, I could tell; after all, we had just left the church and were walking down a path between headstones towards the Rolls. But I was telling him *my* terms, leaving him in no doubt who was to be boss in *my* house. No way was I having him running about drunk at *my* reception, and then slavering and clambering over me on honeymoon… expecting yon.

Daddy had paid for my wedding. Daddy had a good job and gave up his pay packet to mummy each and every Friday night, unopened. I intended to train John that way. I made it plain to him at the reception that when he took over the business he'd not be spending any more takings on booze. My policy was this: if he wanted yon, then he was going to behave. And up to now, he has. Yon, once a month, *if I feel like it*, has kept him in check.

The generally held belief among our circle of friends was that one son and one daughter was 'The gentleman's family'. Accordingly, I instructed John.

In my eyes, my daughter, Morag, was a girl who had university potential. She certainly had the O levels to qualify. Jim had no brains, I was sure, but he was tall, handsome, wore tight jeans, which always had a disgusting bulge in them when he was with Morag. Morag, silly girl, fell head-over-heels for him. She lost concentration and as soon as Jim's apprenticeship finished they married, and away they went to sea together, quite blithely. It troubled me that he was in the 'Merch' and not the 'Royal', but I had no regrets when I learned Morag sat with Jim at the Captain's table on the ship. I took pride in telling the neighbours where Morag was. 'This week she will be in Sydney. Next week she will be in the Fijian Islands, basking in the sun on some exotic beach, pampered by servants.'

Then Morag flies home all tearful and pregnant... it was such a shock, and I hid her from the neighbours.

'You'll have to get Jim home for good, now,' I told her. 'You can't have him gallivanting all over the high seas without keeping an eye on him. There are all those worrying tales of what sailors get up to in port to consider.' I reminded her forcibly of that. 'And he could possibly come home with a....'

It's unmentionable, but he's still there doing his roaming. Morag has not the hold on him that I have on her father. It's evident that the youth of today are far too free with yon. Now, it seems, she has regressed a generation towards John's side of the family... and is sneaking drink indoors. It's evident now that Jim has become a waster who wants no responsibility whatsoever. In my mind, he's becoming the Rab C Nesbitt of the high seas.

The Wife:

'Morag, I'm going to take you down to the sea in ships.' I thought Jim's words were so romantic, and I loved him to bits when I heard them. And I lived and loved the life of Reilly with him. When he took me away on the ship, it was like endless cruising. On moonlit nights on the Pacific Ocean, we'd watch for shooting stars. On days of cloudless skies when the sea was like a mirror, we looked for flying fish skimming the surface and pods of dolphins playing around the ship. Every day I sunbathed on deck and swam in the small swimming pool.

Our Asian steward treated me like a lady. I never had to do a hands turn for two years. I never picked up a duster or an iron, and dirty clothes just disappeared and came back laundered. I sat at the Captain's table to eat. The food was always of good quality, sometimes exotic, and there was plenty of it. I couldn't afford to put on menus the likes of that at home once a day, never mind thrice.

Looking back, life at sea was bliss with Jim. We visited Hawaii and many of the smaller Pacific Islands where we still have friends. I certainly never wanted to return home when Jim's company offered him leave. Encouraged him to stay, I did, and cruised around the world twice.

Jim and I planned that he'd stay at sea, me with him, until we'd saved enough to buy our own home, outright. Then, he'd come ashore and look for a job. Jim said he was up for that, though I had my doubts; he's a lot like his Dad and I know he loves being at sea. Then, I got pregnant.

Things changed quickly and Jim's company insisted I leave the ship at the next port of call and fly home. We had a tearful parting and I wanted Jim home too… right away.

That was a month ago, but now Jim has turned stubborn and doesn't see my side of the argument. He thinks as well as having the bairn, all the other responsibilities of parenthood are down to me, too. Now he says he'll come home in his own good time. Neither my meddlesome mother nor I can push him into making that decision. I can't understand his aversion to being at home with the bairn and me. He thinks I'll come between him and a night out with his pals, but I won't. I'm sure that he thinks there's some character trait of my mother in me, but there isn't. Henpecking's not for Jim, and there won't be any from me. One day soon, I hope he'll realise that. In the meantime, before I go to bed, I have a wee tipple to mask my dreams of Jim, where he is… and where I could have been with him.

The-Father-in-Law:

I've been told not to say anything…

Poetry

Table of Contents

UNCLE WILL WROTE POETRY

Farmer Thomson

Farmer Thomson was at a loss
He farmed a lonely stead on Lochar Moss
His crops lay rotting in heavy rain
Water was filling every drain
As he made his way across the yard
His wife ran out, waving a card
'John', she said, 'They're going to build us a bathroom at last
Farmer Thomson turned, looking aghast
Wiping his forehead with his cuff
'Wumman', he said, 'Dae ye no think oo'r watt enough.

STALKING STICKLEBACKS

(THEN... AND NOW)

Then, the burn trickled its way
Clearly over sandy beds, by lush
Banks, through farmer's fields to
The sea. Beneath the bridge,
Shading the bubble-filled deepening,

Behind the stony cataract where
Sticklebacks, our make-believe
Salmon, were difficult catches,
Wellie wearers using jam jars
Succeeded with low-tech tackle.

The meander through Old Tom's
Meadow offered clear, shallow water,
Where fish darted, hid, gills panicky,
Beneath reedy banks. The fumbling
Touch of the fisherman's hand, so

White, dragged beneath the weeds,
Stirred terror in the wriggling fish.
Threshing minutely, flashing silver,
Creating small ripples, fish started
Towards the low-tech tackle,

Sitting, mouths upstream, awaiting
Fantasy salmon, bog-eyed, magnified,
Confused, to peer through its bottom

Into water trickling clearly over sandy
Beds, by lush banks, to the sea through

Farmer's fields. Now slurry and
Fertilizers pollute the water, killing
Fishing grounds, burdening the burn's
Bed with A jungle of growth
In which sticklebacks cannot live.

GRAVEYARD SHIFTY

Around the headstones of our forefathers,
Uncaring for the dead, we flitted
Silent like the dates of death we never read.

The minister's orchard, beyond the graveyard wall,
Filled with fruit and ripe; ready to fall like the sick
Of his Thursday afternoon visits.

Eyes eager, hungry we await his departure, satchels
Empty, space for scrumping. Nerves shake
The trees; the fruit drops thumping.

Biting to the cores, they're bitter and there's stones.
Rumbling tummies; Mum's appalled, the doctor's summoned.
Cripes! Will the minister pay the final call?

BOYS IN THE MIRE

We boys, forever messing around
On the council tip, our holy ground.
Dodging authority's eyes and the boulders,
We took a lot on our childhood shoulders.

With saw and axe, we cut the planks
Into neat lengths and handy bundles.
With pram wheeled frames, our tanks,
Around wifie's doors, sticks we'd trundle.

Till late at night, with noses runny,
We worked hard for the extra money.
Fit from toil and feeling limber,
Grand it was selling kindling timber,

Until the cop and gaffer came along;
That's when it all went wrong.
It's the nick for you, naughty boys,
We'll teach you there to play with toys.

SENSE OF HAPPINESS

He sounds happy, laughs like thunder
Are all his faculties there, I wonder?
And looking happy he drags me in
Then he kicks me on the shin.
He smells happy? I believe that not,
Must be whiffs of Tommyrot.
He tastes happy? Oh come along.
Now you're just having me on.

NELLIE DENE TO DAVY JONES

The Nellie Dene, her timbers sprung,
Rides deep Beaufort's whooping gale force eleven.

White horses saddling her decks whip to spume.
Eyelessly, they watch her death throes.

Her silver haul jettisons skywards
Spiralling towards the seagull's screams.

The sickening plunge from a wave top beckons
And Davy Jones takes her beneath the oily green.

Short Sketches

Table of Contents

Sketch 1

Characters:
Foreman.
Woman.

The scene is the inside a portacabin on a building site, the office of the hard-hatted foreman. A burly woman dressed in overalls and Wellingtons enters and adopts a manly pose. The foreman is busy poring over some plans spread out on a desk. He looks up and speaks.

FOREMAN: DISINTERESTEDLY: Yes?

WOMAN: I'm looking for a job. I can do any job that man can do.

FOREMAN: LOOKING DOUBTFULLY AT THE WOMAN: What qualifications do you have to do a man's work?

WOMAN: HACKLES RISING: I can work like a horse.

FOREMAN: DISPARAGEMENT EVIDENT IN HIS VOICE: Okay, but can you Pass solids whilst walking?

Sketch 2

Characters:

Wife.

Husband.

The scene is a pleasantly-furnished living-room in a quality home. A husband and the wife are sitting quietly reading newspapers. The husband both acts and speaks down to earth. The wife is bejewelled, dressed very smartly, speaks poshly and gives an air of superiority. She turns a page and speaks.

Wife: I think I'll apply for this job at The Body Shop.

Husband: Make sure you have the qualifications; otherwise, it will be a waste of time.

The wife crashes the paper closed.

Wife, LOUDLY: There you go again, always putting me down. Of course, I have the necessary qualifications. I have intellect. The hands hanging on the ends of my wrists are the most capable in this town for working in a body shop.

The husband shrugs knowingly. The wife reopens the newspaper, writes down the telephone number, then phones, asking for an application form.

Some days later, a letter arrives. The wife opens it and begins to dance round the furniture, joyous at the offer of the job.

Wife, GLEEFULLY AND REPEATEDLY: I've got the job down the body shop.

The wife leaves for her first day at work, dressed to kill, returning home, the wife looks glum.

Husband: How did it go?

Wife, UNHAPPILY AND LETHARGICALLY: I don't think I'll ever get used to   working at the undertakers.

Sketch 3

Characters:

Wife.

Husband.

The scene is the interior of a motor car driven by the husband, along a road winding through an industrial estate. A gasometer appears ahead of the car. The husband leans over, removes a spring-loaded clothes peg from the glove compartment and clips it onto his nose.

Wife, LOOKING QUESTIONINGLY AT HER HUSBAND: What's the idea of that?

Husband, NASALLY AND NODDING KNOWINGLY TOWARDS HIS WIFE: You say you never fart, but I suspect that each time we've passed gasworks recently, you've let one go.

Wife, LOOKING DAGGERS: That's a terrible accusation to make. You must be smelling the reek from the gas works.

Husband, LOOKING DEAD AHEAD, AGAIN NASALLY AND NODDING KNOWINGLY: Really, the gasworks closed down in 1956.

Sketch 4

Characters:

Boy.

Father.

The scene is a farmyard. A number of turkeys, making lots of turkey noises, are chasing a young boy round the yard. The boy's father rides into the farmyard on a tractor and cuts the engine. The boy rushes up to his father and breathlessly speaks.

Boy: Dad, Dad, I don't like the noises these turkeys make. They're scaring me.

Father, WITH A RUEFUL SMILE: Never mind, son. When you grow up (pause)   you'll love the sound of a gobble.

THE BOY LOOKS UP AT HIS FATHER, PUZZLED.

Sketch 5

Characters:
Famous footballer.
Supporter 1.
Supporter 2.

The scene is after the game, outside Ibrox stadium. (any stadium) Rangers (team associated with stadium) have lost at home and two diehard supporters, bedecked with club bunting, have waited outside, building up their confidence to assault verbally the players as they leave.

Supporter 1: I'll give them what fur, the haddies.

Supporter 2: Aye, me and ah.

Supporter 1: They were a load o' rubbish the day!

Supporter 2: Aye, yer right.

Team manager (famous footballer) walks through a door carrying a hefty tree trunk.

Supporter 1: SHOUTS: It's good to see you take some stick, Ally.

BOTH SUPPORTERS TURN AND WALK SWIFTLY AWAY.

Supporters 1 and 2 together: We telt him, didn't we.

Sketch 6

Characters:
Wedding party.
Bride.
Groom.

Scene 1: A white wedding.

The young, virginal-looking bride, in conversation with her ladies in waiting, mentions the size of her husband's manhood.
The best man is making suggestive actions to the groom: giving him the short arm sign.

Wife: COYLY TO SEVERAL WOMEN FRIENDS: I just can't wait to get my big boy into bed. I haven't seen it yet, but he must have the largest penis in Scotland.

Ladies in waiting: ONE TO THE OTHER, CATTILY: She wouldn't know what to do with it.

Scene 2: HONEYMOON SUITE:

The bride is sitting in the bed watching her husband undress. We see the back of the husband standing naked, and the bride pointing to his crotch area.

Wife: RATHER DISAPPOINTEDLY: When you first began writing to me, you said you had 'at least a foot'.

Husband: SOUNDING HURT: I said I had 'athlete's foot', but you've never mentioned your dyslexia.

Sketch 7

Characters:

Mary.

Paddy.

The scene is a street on a Dublin housing estate. It is 21:00 hours on a Saturday. a housewife dressed in a pinafore, leaves a house and runs along a pavement in her slippered feet. She opens the door of a telephone kiosk, enters and dials a number. Behind a bar in a busy pub, a telephone rings. The woman's husband, Paddy, a barman, picks up the phone.

Woman, IN A BROAD DUBLIN ACCENT, SPEAKS INTO THE PHONE: Is that you, Paddy?

Paddy, QUICKLY: Aye, and I thought I told you never to phone me at work?

Woman: Ach aye, ah know, but it's important.

Paddy: What is it then?

Woman: Er…er, I've got some bad news for you, some worse news, but at the end of the day, the news isn't so bad at all, at all.

Paddy: Bayjasus, tell me the bad news?

Woman: You remember those six lottery numbers you asked me to put on this afternoon?

Paddy, BEGINNING TO GUESS WHAT'S COMING, PULLS A FACE: Aye, I do.

Woman, FUSSING WITH HER HEADSQUARE: Silly me, I forgot to put them on.

Paddy, STANDING UP STRAIGHT, EXPECTING A SHOCK: Sufferin' Jasus, what's the worse news?

197

Woman, BLURTS OUT: All six numbers came out tonight.

Paddy, BEGINNING TO FUME, SHOUTS: Bayjasus, what can the better news be, after me hearing that?

Woman, CHEERFULLY: Ach, there's little to worry about, there was no winners!

Paddy picks up the phone and throws it through a window.

And Finally Some More Poetry

Table of Contents

BURN ME UP AXEMAN

Doglegs tripping me on my road through life,
Led me into this town, this deadly strife.
In its unlit streets, I found darker places,
Mary Jane and other bitches to untie my laces.

That morning, the mists they're calling,
Rolling in to kill my brain.
Feeling it's over as I keep falling,
No recovery from that final pain.

Along the road axeman, play that riff.
Ramp it up with a five-bar shift.
Play it high.
Swing it low.
Play it long when you see the glow.
Sing along with the devil's choir.
Jack it up as I hit the fire,
Smoke and sparks spewing from my burning pyre.

My mind went numb, it hit the spot.
A bad fix, from a bad lot.
Take care back there if you fear what you see,
My advice from eternity.

Along the road axeman, play that riff.
Ramp it up with a five-bar shift.
Play it higher.
Swing it lower
Rock it slowly, just once more.
Letting it rip as I hit the fire.
Keep it going till there is no ire,
Nothing left of me but ash in that smoking, stinking pyre.

FLYAWAY LOVER

When you said the words I love you
You tempted me with your lies
The twinkle has gone, never was true
Flashing from your lovely, starling-egg-blue eyes

Songbirds singing in the evening time
Calling for mates with a musical chime
Reminder for me of the feelings I once had
Not fearing for a love-match yet to turn bad

Our love had reached the gates of hell
Quickly over, it has descended
Passing through that fiery veil
To where it cannot be mended

It's over now; will life ever be the same?
The time I spent with you I think a crying shame
What I'd given, I'll find hard to recover
It's what you get on discovering a worthless lover

Songbirds singing in the evening time
Calling for mates with a musical chime
Reminder for me of the feelings I once had
Not fearing for a love-match yet to turn bad

MYSTERY TOUR

When I could not resist your lure
You took me on a mystery tour
The magician working your devious mind
Tricked me and was so unkind.

You had me easily falling
Your sexy voice had that calling
Took me in, made me insecure
A lonely lad, so immature.

My mind, you took for a scenic drive
To places too mystical to contrive
Devilish places with no detour
How possibly could I resist your lure?

It beats me now, how I went along
Listening to your siren song
Words for which there was no cure
Thoughts I now know were so impure.

Now that I am happily apart
I can look back at your evil art
How easily you took me in
Put my mind in a fiendish spin.

Snake charming

She was a snake, danger in her fangs
She lay in wait; she'd not regret your pangs
Fork tongue leading, she struck out.
Lies for the telling, she went down that route
She dragged me in with bags of leading,
Where's my weak spot, she'd been probing
Seeking out with malice, she'd umbrage on her stall,
The strike was good, there's no escape and I'd taken it all.

You were no cobra girl, just a sneaky adder
A diamond back on the make,
You thought you'd make me madder
Get off your belly now, you'll never make me madder.
Get off your belly now, you'll never make me sadder

Venom from her hellish soul, she injected
Numbed my brain, where my thoughts collected
I used to love her very much, but now it's all spat out
Lips she's frozen I cannot move I am a soundless nut.
I cannot say I love her now, cornered in this cranny
Her power over me was just a bit uncanny
I recovered quickly, broke out, got over the doping.
She'd hit me good; finally to be free, is what I'm hoping.

You were no cobra girl, just a sneaky adder
A diamond back on the make,
You thought you'd make me madder
Get off your belly now, you'll never make me madder.
Get off your belly now, I've never felt much gladder

THE EYE OF THE HURRICANE

The eye of the hurricane is making landfall tonight
It's centre blasts code red, we're all in for a fright
Seas are surging, waves breaking over the land
Rock music couldn't match the roar, no need for a band

The waters are rising, breaking over my heart
The storm levies are filling, keeping us apart
The winds are tugging; lifting, hijacking all we knew
Leaving me with memories, all those memories of you
You made me so blue, blue, blue,
Couldn't get over you, you, you,
The wind is spiralling high, high, high,
Is this our last goodbye, eye, eye……..goodbye

The winds are howling, on the edge of hell I stand
To put to bed my demons, there is no magic wand
If you don't come back to me, what's the use of prayer
You've blown me out; done the job of a heartless slayer.

The circling storm is boiling around you, sun and stars dim
together,
Tall like the night and twisting, keeping your eye on the weather
Your love for me is dying; in its final throes, It leaves a leaden heat
The rock band has started pounding, no relief from its beat

You made me so blue, blue, blue,
Couldn't get over you, you, you,
The wind is spiralling high, high, high,
Is this our last goodbye, eye, eye……..goodbye
Is this our last goodbye?

204

Tom Tom

Tom, Tom let me feel your touch
Your rhythm that I like so much
You reached me with your beat
Leaving me gasping on Drum-roll Street
Tickled my skin, let the sequence in
Wrapped me up in a woolly bearskin

Hot was the night when you struck up
Music flowing, without letup
Arms flashing wildly, moving air
The beat moving me from despair
Cymbals rattling, ringing a bell
Keeping me from my date with hell

Drums, their beat had that calling
Bowled me over, saw me falling
The tender way you stroked my skin
Put me in that bewildering backspin

Hot was the night when you struck up
Arms flashing wildly, moving air
The beat moving me from despair
Music flowing without letup
Cymbals rattling, ringing a bell
Keeping me from my date with hell

Saga of the Lost Kecks

The mystery was never solved
Though around my trousers, it involved
Where they went, I do not know
They weren't there, where did they go?

They aren't an ordinary pair of slacks
Ones that hung on tailor's racks
But strides ahead of their time
Swaddling for my legs sublime

A pair of shiny, distinguished trews
That went well with brown brogue shoes
They've gone like big bits of my mind
Please bring them back, if you'd be so kind

This pair of brown, corduroy pants
A present from two favourite aunts
Will I ever find to wear again?
For I cannot be seen in breeks so plain

Attached to them were belt and braces
Keeping them up, they were my aces
The metal zip to padlock the fly
Gave speedier access to my inner thigh

I will admit that one dark night
Caught short, I stopped in dire plight
Behind a tree, released for a dump
Did the kecks get grubby; was I a chump?

Walking home, with trousers discarded
I must have looked a wee bit retarded
But in that state, my loss less unexplained
I'm feeling happier, not looking so pained

BOXED SET

Several of my mates aren't around anymore
Boxed up, boxed up
They lie below together all togged up
Boxed up, boxed up
Drugs they took were good, they swore
And died sporting the silly grins they wore
Boxed up, boxed up

So the promise of staying clean
I know how my end might have been
Boxed up, boxed up

Gravely now, I view their eternal plots
Boxed up, boxed up
In their short lives, they drew fateful lots
Boxed up, boxed up
On bleak headstones, their stories told
Final words about ones so bold
Boxed up, boxed up

So the promise of staying clean
My early end and how it might have been
Boxed up, boxed up
I know how my end might have been
Boxed up, boxed up

Falling from grace

Graveyards of my childhood were emptier then
Fuller now; coffins filled with dead friends
Lads I used to know, going way too far
Chasing the dragon on a Saturday night, blew their minds ajar.

Letting in the demons, they'd turned to hard drugs
Bought from friends, who'd turned out thugs
Peddling from street corners and any shady passage
They cared not their friend's end would be so savage.

Walking around standing headstones, there's room for more
Falling from grace an option I'm not keen to explore
The false lure of angels dancing, I will not take the gamble
Erstwhile friend's sale pitches were just a preamble.

DREAM TRAVELLING

Far off horizons,
Where travel takes me.
I reach there alone,
Without you.
How I wish you were with me;
Sharing my dreams,
These far off places,
Marvelling over each strange sounding name.

I told you I would fly,
Away high.
Now I've flown,
Away on my own,
And you must wonder,

If I will miss you,
On Cloudless nights,
A multitude of stars
Looking down on me.
If I cry to the full moon,
When I need a little madness,
Amidst all the sadness,
Of missing you, day after day.

I told you I would fly,
Away high.
Now I've flown,
Away on my own.
And do you wonder why?

Do you wonder why ?

Printed in Great Britain
by Amazon